The year is 1928. Jenny Couling lives at Holly
Bank. Farm in Gloucestershire with her father
Garnett, two brothers, Jacob and Giles, and a
dog, named Dog. Her mother disappeared four
years earlier because of Garnett's cruelty. Now
it seems Jenny must suffer the same cruelty
from her father and elder brother Jacob. But
she proves to be a stronger person than she
originally thought, and with the help of her
close friend, Chas Hanks, overcomes many
trials and tribulations and strives
to move on.

*To Madona
Best wishes
Max 26 april 2007
Wyman.*

My thanks to Anita, Liam & Conor for
their support & to Ruth without who
I would not have been able to
produce this book.

# Dark Secrets

A first novel by

# Max Ryman

\*\*\*

Edited by Ruth Durnin

ISBN 978-1-84753-082-0

# DARK   SECRETS


## PART   ONE


## ONE


Shafts of light pierced through the split in her bedroom window as Jenny

yawned and opened her eyes. She already sensed it was well past six o'clock,

her normal time for rising. She knew why she had overslept. That was easy. Her

father had beaten her the night before, and as a result, she needed sleep to

recover. But what had caused her to wake up now. A noise, a sense, a being.

She was not sure.

She lay there motionless, between the cotton sheets. The top sheet crushed

tightly between her hands; bruised and swollen like her lips. She listened, but

could hear nothing.

Outside one of the milking cows lowed from the cowshed; eager to be milked.

Would that have awakened her? She thought not. Although she felt guilty for

not having drawn the milk from the cow and her four companions.

It was the middle of winter and the weak sun outside was not yet warming the

day. She shivered in the bed and strained her ears for any further sounds.  She

heard footsteps leading down the stairs; and knew her elder brother Jacob was making his way down to the parlour. She should have been up long ago. She should have milked the cows and had the breakfast table set for her men folk. Three men, with her the only female. A beast of a father, who beat her whenever the fancy took him. An elder brother who had many of his father's traits. And young Giles. Just twelve years old and a pleasure to be with. But just like her, scared of the two other members of their family.

A searing pain shot through her body. From the front of her belly to the spine. It lasted only a few seconds, but enough to make her arch her back in agony. Was that the reason for her waking now? An earlier spasm. Maybe. She lay there, still, in her bed. Waiting for the next one to come.

She was used to pain. Since her Mother walked out on them when Jenny was no more than twelve years old. The same age that Giles was now. Her Mother had suffered pain at the hands of Garnett Couling. The same pain that Jenny suffered now. But Jenny was still enduring that pain. It had just been transferred to her from her Mother.

Footsteps were approaching, back up the uncarpeted wooden stairs. It was her elder brother. She knew his footsteps instinctively. They were different from her father's. Jacob was a big man, but light on his feet. Surprisingly so. The door flew open without the courtesy of a knock and the frame was filled by Jacob's mighty bulk. He may not have been as tall as their father, but he was not far short.

"Where's our breakfast," he bellowed, striding across the small room. Towering above her, he ripped the top sheet and cover from Jenny's swollen hands; revealing a small, pathetic body laying across the bed, covered in a plain white shift. Looking down at her with piercing eyes, set into a large round face, he studied her body for a few moments; seemingly unaware of any cuts and bruises.

"Well?" he bellowed. "Where is it?"

"I'm bad Jacob," she muttered in barely a whisper.

"Really bad. I need rest."

"Rest be damned," he snarled, grabbing her clothes from a chair near the window.

"We all need rest. But there's work to be done."

"Here, put these on," he snarled, throwing the bundle across her body.

"And don't take long about it."

For a few seconds he stared down at her. His eyes lost their fierce piercing stare and there was something else about them. Something she had seen occasionally over the past few months. She had no idea what it meant. How could she. Being only sixteen and living on a small farm near Gloucester, she was not worldly to such things. She had a lot to learn.

Suddenly, and without warning, he turned. The light coming through the window caught the side of his face. He towered above her; like a giant. Then he was gone. And she was left alone. Quiet. Save for the sound of his leather boots disappearing down the wooden stairs.

She trembled violently and could not control herself. Every sinew, every nerve in her body, cried out in pain. She needed rest. She needed sleep. So very much. To sleep, and heal her body and her mind. To forget, just for a moment, this hell hole in which she lived. This so called home.

# TWO

Creeping silently down the stairs, her small white feet, bare now, making less noise than the mouse that scurried across the step, a yard or so in front of her, she clutched the banister with one hand and held her belly with the other. The pain came and went like waves. She wanted to cry out; to release the tension welling up inside. But she knew it was best not to. Remain quiet; that was the answer. So the men in her life would not know she was there. Save for Giles. Dear Giles. Where would he be? She had no idea of the time. He may still be in his bed. In the room alongside hers. Which he shared with Jacob. Or he may be at school. Or downstairs, like the other two, in the parlour, waiting for his breakfast. Dear God, she hoped not. He mustn't see her like this. Not again, like he had so many times before. He was only twelve, bless him. He should not be subjected to seeing his sister like this.

Lifting the latch half way up the door she entered the parlour to be greeted by three pairs of eyes. One pair was indifferent. That was Garnett, her father. He seemed to be unaware that he inflicted pain on his women folk. One pair was of anger; the other of love.

"Are you all right Jenny?" asked Giles, rising from his chair, about to greet her.

"'course she's all right," snapped his father, slapping a huge hand onto the boy's arm, forcing him back into his seat.

"She's overslept, that's all. Ain't you, Jen?"

She nodded slightly as every sinew in her neck grew taught. Giving the merest hint of a smile to her younger brother, she scurried past him and across the parlour, stoking the fire, set in the black cast iron range. Fortunately there were still a few embers glowing from the previous night of merriment. With a prod of the poker here and a prod there they soon sparkled back into life. The old black kettle was half filled with water and placed on top of the range, and slowly she prepared breakfast.

Her father and two brothers remained seated around the table discussing what plans they had for the day. Giles said very little. Whenever the opportunity arose he would turn towards Jenny, eager to catch her eye. To show his sister that he cared for her. But whether she sensed it or not, she was always looking away.

"I'll be at market most of the day," grunted Garnett, between puffs on his pipe. "After I've taken milk to the creamery. We need a couple of young heifers to calve in the spring. They mightn't be too dear this time of year."

Without taking her eyes from the eggs she was frying, Jenny breathed a sigh of relief. With her father away for the day she would have time to rest. To begin the recovery period. To relax. There was a downside though. There was every chance that after a days heavy drinking at the market he would come home drunk. Slightly drunk; if she was lucky. Or so drunk that he would be in a fowl

mood again. Like last night. But she had to think on the bright side. At least she

had a day's grace. A day she could be by herself.

Jacob's deep gruff voice interrupted her thoughts.

"What d'you want me to do?" he asked, tapping his knife impatiently against

the wooden table, heavily scarred from years of family life.

Garnett blew a mouthful of spent tobacco smoke across the room.

"I want you earning your keep lad" he said.

"Old Zack at The Nags Head has got a leaking roof. You're not bad at tiling. I

told him you'd go over and give him a hand."

Jacob smiled. It would give him some time off from the farm. And he had

taken a fancy to Zack's daughter already. Even though she didn't seem to feel

the same way for him.

Jenny smiled too. But not so they could see. With Jacob away for the day as

well, she would have the farm to herself. She would have liked Giles to be with

her. She felt almost secure with him around; in a strange sort of way. Maybe he

was only twelve. But he seemed older at times. When they were together. And a

cuddle from him would always perk her up. But he still had his schooling to

think about. And one thing she was determined of was a good education for

him. So he could make his way in the world. If he could read and write he

would get on. She was sure of that.

"Where's our breakfast, girl?" bellowed Garnett, breaking into his daughter's thoughts.

"We ain't got all day, you know."

Leaning back in his carver chair he picked a lump of dirt from beneath his finger nail with a fingernail on the other hand. Giles watched in silence. Already from Jenny he had learnt the basic art of hygiene. At least he washed his hands before a meal. Not like his father. Who allowed dirt and grime to build up on his 'till it was grained in.

"Coming Dad," whispered Jenny, struggling across the parlour with three plates; one in each hand, and one resting on her arm. She was so professional at this balancing trick from years of practice with her family that she could easily have served as a waitress in one of the posh tea rooms in Gloucester. At least, that was what she had been told by Gladys, one of her few friends who lived in the nearby town of Lechlade. And the money wasn't too bad either.

Two thirds of a loaf of bread and a plate of butter came next, followed by cups of steaming hot tea. Then Jenny found her shoes and a shawl and made her way to the back door.

"You not eating with us then, Jen?" asked her father, his mouth full with a lump of bacon and egg, oblivious to the plight of his daughter.

"I'll milk the cows first," she said in little more than a whisper. "I'll have mine when I come back in."

"Good girl," chuckled Garnett, shoveling more food onto an empty fork. "As my old dad used to say, God rest his soul; you should always feed your stock afore you feed yourself. An' he weren't too far wrong."

Not really the reason for Jenny's departure though. She needed time alone. To think, to relax. Think what she could do with her life; how to escape. And what better place to do that than alone in the cowshed, along with the five milking cows. The cold winters air bit into her hard as she crossed the yard, and she pulled her late granny's shawl tighter around her small frail body. Her leather shoes, made by a local cobbler in Lechlade, did little to keep her feet warm. But they were better than nothing. As she entered the cowshed she was struck by the heat generated from the cattle inside and it warmed her. A complete contrast to the cold of the snow outside. And the smell of hay; a smell that she would remember for the rest of her life. As she closed the door the cows turned their heads in recognition. Their udders were full of milk and the teats were leaking from two of them. They were uneasy and she knew it. Lighting an oil lamp and hanging it to a nail placed high in the wall, she fed the first of her charges with a scoop of grain. Grabbing a three legged stool and a bucket, she sat down and pushed her head deep into the animal's flank, before pulling on the teats to extract a gallon and a half of warm fresh milk. The large roan beast would constantly flick her tail across Jenny's face, more from habit than annoyance. But she took little notice this morning. Other things were on her mind.

9

## THREE

Garnett Couling had already delivered his churn of milk to the creamery. He was late, but no one held that against him. And nor would they. Very few men in the county had the gall to upset him. He was a hard man, and bred to the land. He had been brought up and gained respect the hard way; and that's how he liked it.

Having dropped Jacob off at The Nags Head in Buscot to help out with the leaking roof, he was now steering the battered old Austin pick up truck off the main road and into Fairford cattle market. A couple of farmers raised their hand as he passed in his search for a space amongst the vehicles already parked there, and he raised his own in acknowledgment. It would be a busy market, and he cursed aloud. A lot of customers often meant high prices, and he wanted to buy cheap. It was so busy; in fact, they were housing cattle in The Croft, an area just off the High Street, which the drovers made use of when the other pens in Market Place and The High Street were full. He cursed again. But this time at his daughter. It was her fault. She had made him late. He would put her in her place tonight. Make her remember the next time.

An old couple in a bone shaker, that belched great plumes of blue smoke from its exhaust, trundled past as they vacated a parking slot. Either the steering wheel was loose or the old fellow had no control over the use of his hands, for the narrow wheels at the front of the vehicle suddenly turned to the right, bounced towards Garnett's motor, and only but for the grace of God was there was no collision. With a blast on his horn Garnett swore through the open window and told the driver that he was a stupid old bugger and should never be allowed near a car; and the best place for him was a lunatic asylum. If the old fellow heard him, which he probably didn't, because he was partially deaf, he showed no sign. He was far more interested in struggling with the steering wheel and the safety of his wife.

When they were gone Garnett parked up and tied his dark grey lurcher to the corner stay of the pick up. He took Dog everywhere he went. He was an ugly creature. A large dog; but an ugly dog. A wall eye to the right of his face and half an ear to the left. Probably bitten off by another vicious creature long before he arrived at the Couling homestead. That was three years ago. Much the same sort of day as today. Except that the sun wasn't shining. True, it was the middle of winter. But a cold, dank miserable day. One of those days when you wish that spring was here, but you know deep down that it's a long way off. He just arrived early one morning. In the yard. A stray. Probably lost, and nowhere to go. So he chose Holly Bank Farm. It was as simple as that. Garnett never did try and trace his owner. Certainly never mentioned it to the local copper. He had no time for the law anyway. Best to keep well away from them that was his motto. Garnett had always called him Dog. Just hadn't got round to thinking of a proper name for him. That's all. But it did no harm. The animal still responded to the name Dog whenever Garnett shouted at him. And they seemed to like each others company.

"Stay there, you bugger" swore Garnett as the dog whined when his master walked away.

"And you can stop that bloody whimpering as well," he added, giving the old creature a box around the ears.

A well to do woman dressed in tweed with a small child latched to her arm glanced at the scruffy farmer and then at his dog as she passed them by.

"And what's your problem, Missus?" he asked, searching for a match to light his pipe.

"You got nothin' better to do than worry about a bloody ol' dog."

The woman pulled the young boy closer to her and scurried off down a narrow passageway that led to Fairford's main shopping area. Garnett chuckled, lit his pipe and joined another local farmer making his way over to the auction ring.

"Not a bad day," said the farmer.

"Not bad at all," agreed Garnett. "Could be a bloody sight worse."

"And ain't that a fact," replied the farmer.

The two men walked on.

"So, what would you be after today then?" he asked. "Or you just out here for the pleasure."

Garnett laughed.

"That'll be the day when I come out just for pleasure." He said. " All I ever seem to do is work; morning, noon and night. Just to keep body and soul together."

"You poor old bugger," chuckled the other man, slapping a black and white cow on the rump as a drover chivied her past.

"You seemed to be enjoying yourself all right last night," he said, referring to a late night drinking session at The Bull Inn the previous night.

"Ah," grunted Garnett. "That were different. I'd had a skin full, I was in good company, and decided to make the best of it. That were all."

"You did that all right," replied the other man. "Not seen you so pissed for a long time."

"And ain't that the truth," laughed Garnett, slapping the other man heartily on the back as they made their way through the cattle pens, many still full with animals, waiting for their turn in the auction ring.

# FOUR

Jenny had long since milked the cows, fed and watered the geese and chicken,

collected the eggs, cleaned the bedrooms and laid fresh sheets across the beds.

Now she was bottle feeding one of the two orphan lambs in the parlour, in front

of the cooking range. With the lamb laid across her lap, guzzling greedily from

the teat, she used her spare hand to stroke its woolly back. Soft and wrinkly it

was now. Nothing like it would turn into as the lamb grew older and rejoined

the flock. But that was a while off yet. And Jenny was grateful for its company.

Like that of its sibling, now asleep in the cardboard box, with a full belly and

maybe a head full of dreams.

Jenny had dreams. Many dreams. Many were frightening. In fact, most were

frightening. Bad, bad nightmares. Of her father. Thrashing her, doing terrible

things to her. Of Jacob, looking on. Sometimes drawing close. Sometimes just

watching. With that horrible grin and his stained teeth. And she would awake in

the middle of the night. Sweating, breathing in great gulpfulls of air, trembling

and crying. Always crying. Or sobbing. But never loud enough for the rest of

her family to hear.

And occasionally, very occasionally, she would have sweet dreams. Dreams

she would cherish. For a few days at least. Before they disappeared, with the

passing of time, slowly from her mind. Like an early morning mist rolling away across the fields, as the sun slowly rose from its sleep and warmed the earth. For these dreams were dreams of her mother, when she would take Jenny in her arms and cuddle her, play with her, come to her room at night, sit with her and tell stories. Slowly brush her long golden hair before she was tucked up in bed with a goodnight kiss to the cheek. And watch through narrow sleepy eyes as her mother left the room and blow a kiss, before closing the door and making her way down the stairs. Those were the dreams Jenny cherished. Unfortunately, there were not many of them. And as she stroked the lambs small wiry body the tears came to her eyes and rolled softly down her cheeks.

# FIVE

The Nags Head was your typical country pub, set in the middle of Buscot, and built from local sand stone. The current owner, Zack, had lived there all his life; and his father before him, and his father before him too. So you could say as how it was like a family concern. Trouble was, Zack and his wife had only produced one child. Tammy. And that was the trouble. True, she may have been a handsome young girl, with a fine body, a long pair of legs and a strong spirit But she was still a girl. And that didn't bode well on Zack's shoulders. His wish was that The Nags Head would carry on in the same tradition as it had done for the past one hundred and fifty three years. Owned and cared for by the Bosberry family. And as of right now there seemed little chance of that.

Tammy was approaching her twenty fourth year. Zack, having fathered her late in life, him now being sixty three, had little control over her fiery spirit, and although he had tried on various occasions to marry her off to any local lad in the village  who might show an interest in running a nice little pub, she would have none of it. She was determined to stay single, although maybe not a virgin, for the foreseeable future, and was only helping her dad out until he could find someone else to buy the pub off him so he could retire. As for her future, she had that planned. Well, almost. At the first opportunity, she would make her way to the bright lights of London; there to make a career for herself. And a fortune. The trouble was, when anyone asked her what that career would be she didn't quite know the answer. But she knew there was something out there far better than pulling pints behind a bar.

And that's where Jacob ended up. After a hard morning of setting tiles straight on her father's roof, and replacing a few broken ones, he was cold, and eager for some refreshment. Walking into the snug, he felt the heat from the log fire warm his face and he slapped his hands before rubbing them together for extra effect. Walking up to the bar he smiled at Tammy and spoke to her breasts.

"Gorr, you'd warm any man's heart on a day like this, my luv," he laughed, pulling a few coins from his pocket and slapping them on the counter. A man a few feet farther up the bar turned and laughed with him.

"It would take a better man than you, Jacob Couling, to warm my heart," she grinned, turning for a glass, before turning back and pulling a pint.

"Or any part of me, come to that."

He chuckled.

"But you wouldn't mind me giving it a go, would you," he laughed, ignoring the pint of bitter placed before him, still staring at her ample breasts and cleavage, partly covered by a loosely buttoned black cotton blouse.

She took the coins and handed him the change after returning from the till. Leaning forward across the bar, knowing full well he could see far more of her cleavage than he ought to; she smiled and looked deep into his eyes.

"Jacob, if you were the last man on this earth I wouldn't let you near me. When I'm with a man I need to be satisfied." She paused and he was just about to speak. But before he could open his mouth she placed a long pointed index finger against his lips.

"From what I've heard from local girls, my darlin', you ain't got enough down there to satisfy a pigmy. Let alone a full grown girl like me."

With that, she turned, and with a bop of her head, and a chuckle, jauntily walked back through into the other bar. The man at the end of the bar laughed aloud. Jacob turned. His eyes held that vicious look that Jenny had seen earlier in the morning, when he ripped the sheets from her bed.

"You takin' the piss, mister," he asked, squaring up his shoulders in much the same way he did every time he was itching for a fight. The man turned and studied the optics on the wall in front of him. He was only passing through the village and had no desire for any trouble.

"I asked you a question, mister'" snarled Jacob, moving menacingly closer along the bar.

Luckily for the stranger, who was not a large a man, old Zack had just walked . through from the back yard. Having been in the victual trade for all his adult . life, he knew instinctively when trouble was brewing. And he was ready for it now.

"So, Jacob lad," he said, casually, pouring himself half a pint of mild and leaning against the bar.

"How much do I owe you for the roofing job. From what I see, you've done a first class job. Far better than any other lad round these parts could have done."

For a few seconds Jacob continued to stare at the stranger, and Zack wondered whether he had done enough to quell the situation. But by praising the farmer boy he had taken the heat out of the situation and, as Jacob was rarely praised for anything, especially by his father, such praise made him feel as though he was worth something after all.

"A fiver should cover it," he said, looking back into his glass.

Zack thought a fiver was a bit excessive. Especially as the whole job had only taken a couple of hours. But under the circumstances, he felt the best course of action was to pay up and look big. And for two reasons. One, he knew he could never have climbed up onto the roof with his accursed rheumatism and put the job right himself. And secondly, he didn't relish the thought of a fight breaking out in his pub where he would have to end up barring Jacob and footing the bill for the damage. So pay up he did, the stranger left as soon as he got the nod from Zack, and Jacob drank his way through a few more pints that afternoon and was reasonably happy.

# SIX

Garnett worked alone when he was looking for stock to buy. Nothing annoyed him more than having some idiot prattling on about all things under the sun when he was trying to find the merits of a beast he was about to buy. Searching the lines of pens he came across three young heifers. Two were nice lookers; and one should have been put down at birth. That was the roan. The pair of Friesians he could see money in. If he could get them all at the right price. And maybe he could. There was every chance the roan would bring the price of all three down if they were being sold together. And maybe they were.

Calling out to a nearby drover he said "Are these three going as a job lot."

The drover nodded, being more concerned with a contrary old Hereford bull he was herding up to the holding pen.

"And who owns them?" Shouted Garnett as the drover passed.

"Thomas Hignal, from out Buscot way. On the Faringdon road" was the reply as the drover disappeared out of sight.

Garnett was pleased . Hignal was a neighbour of his. All right, not that close a neighbour. Maybe three or four miles past Buscot; and Holly Bank farm was mid way between Buscot and Lechlade. But still close enough. And they had done business in the past. Garnett bought an old blue and white nurse cow from him some years back She had reared over twenty good strong calves from various mothers. Until she had to go to the knackers yard. And Hignal hadn't asked too dear a price for her. But these heifers were already entered in the sale. It was not likely that Garnett would get Hignal to withdraw them. But if there was half a chance he would try.

Now Garnett may have had a temper on him. And not been the best of men to be married to a woman. But still, he knew his livestock. And he knew these three heifers were in calf. But still, just to satisfy himself, as he checked their teeth, their under developed udders and their rumps, he gave each in turn a punch with his fist into the side of the belly, somewhere just before the hip bone. It would be hard to describe the exact place any better than this, for I have known many a so called stockman unable to feel the return bump of an unborn calf as they punched the belly in this manner. But a good stockman can hit the right spot every time, and Garnett was no exception.

Unfortunately, although he found Hignal, he was not prepared to withdraw the heifers from the sale. And Garnett had not found much else suitable. So he had to take his chance like the rest of them. Taking his place alongside the auctioneer, he stood with his elbow resting on the edge of the rostrum, near the auctioneer's foot. When the time came to do the bidding, he merely raised his hand enough to reach the auctioneers coat, and every time he needed to raise the bid, he would gently tug on the coat. No one knew he was bidding, and that was the way he liked it. It was his business, and he had always liked to keep his business to himself.

In actual fact, the sale went in his favour. He paid thirty five pounds for the three, knew he could sell the roan that was only fit for the knackers yard for at least five, which put the nice pair of Friesians in at fifteen pounds a piece. Plus a bit of buyers commission to the auctioneer. Not bad, considering he would have paid twenty to twenty five apiece in a private deal with Hignal. Not bad at all.

With a few spare bob in his pocket, after paying off the auctioneer, and young Chas Hanks to deliver them to Holly Bank Farm, he made his way to The Bull Inn, a regular haunt of his.

# SEVEN

By the time Giles arrived home from school, that Wednesday afternoon, Jenny had been thinking a great deal about her life. Not that she had made too many decisions, but certainly done a great deal of thinking. And uppermost in her mind now was how she could leave Holly Bank Farm. There was just the germ of an idea there at the moment. For Jenny was not too bright. She had a good heart. Was kind to both people and animals. But it took a little while for more than one or two good ideas to form in her mind at the same time. Giles on the other hand, was very bright. He was full of life, enjoyed school, was a quick learner, and loved coming home to tell Jenny all that he had done during the day.

Pulling his satchel from his back and throwing it onto the table, he accepted a mug of hot broth from Jenny and the two of them pulled up a chair each to study his work that day. As usual, Jenny gave him a great deal of praise. Whether she understood all he said or showed her was immaterial, for she had not received the best of educations. Garnett didn't believe in girls reading fancy books and things. Their place was in the home, looking after their men folk. And even though her mother had tried to persuade him otherwise, it had little effect. And sometimes, if she picked the wrong time to disagree with him, it could lead to a beating.

When Giles finally calmed down he began slowly reading a book about the British Empire. It fascinated him; the stories and the pictures of other countries. Of the different peoples, their cultures and their religions. There were not too many words he didn't understand, and those he didn't he just ignored.

"Would you like to travel, Giles?" asked Jenny, in such a way as not to show too much interest.

"Oh yes," he replied excitedly. "Can you just imagine, Jen? Seeing people and places like this in real life. It would be wonderful. Just wonderful, wouldn't it?"

"I suppose so," she answered casually, placing a bowl of milk on the range and  warming it for the twin lambs, still snuggled up in their box. She knew they would wake soon. They always did. They seemed to sense when she was boiling the milk. And although she knew it was time for their feed, she still wanted a few more reactions from her brother.

"Suppose so!"

He almost yelled, turning round in his chair to face her.

"Suppose so. It would be a chance in a lifetime. You just couldn't afford to miss it if it came along."

"Maybe for you," she smiled, watching the first of the bubbles break the skin on the milk as it began to simmer. "It's all right for boys. But it's not the sort of things girls do. Especially country girls like me."

"That's rubbish, and you know it," retorted Giles, acting far more mature than he should have been at twelve.

"Is it?" she asked, pouring the milk into a baby's bottle and placing a teat over the end.

"Of course it is," he replied.

"Everyone should be allowed to travel. Whether it's a man, a woman, a boy or a girl. Nobody should hold us back."

She chuckled.

"What are you laughing at?" he asked, the first signs of a frown furrow forming across his brow.

She shook her head slowly from side to side, then walked over to him. After placing the bottle on the table, she placed her arms around his neck and kissed his cheek from behind.

"Oh Giles," she whispered. "My dear Giles. You have such wonderful ideas. And I hope you keep them. And I hope they come true for you. I really do. But do you honestly think I'll ever be in a position to leave this place?"

"And why not?" he asked, cupping her hands in his, and looking at the deep crisp snow out through the parlour window.

"You're as good as anyone else. Better in fact, as far as I'm concerned."

"Maybe," she sighed.

"Maybe. But I can't see Dad ever letting me leave. Can you? Not while he hasn't got a woman around to take my place."

Releasing her hands he pulled them apart, stood up and turned to face her.

"Then we'll run away," he said, as though he had made the most straight forward decision in his life.

"We'll run away together and leave the two of them to get on the best they can. It's as simple as that."

For a moment she stared into his soft brown eyes, and saw there the love that only a boy can hold for his sister. True love; the love that no one can ever take away. Unrequited love. So different from Jacob. So very different.

She shook her head.

"If only it was that simple. If only we could pack up and go."

Now she held him in her arms and pulled him tightly to her.     He looked up at her and for a moment she felt he was a man. A fully grown man, albeit small for his age. But one who would take care of her. Forever. For the rest of her life. But all too soon she came back to reality as she heard footsteps on the stones outside the back door. Footsteps she recognized. Jacob had returned home.

Swiftly releasing her grip on Giles she turned, grabbed the bottle of milk and hurried to the range. Giles, somewhat unsure of his feelings, turned to face the door, waiting for his brother to enter. For a moment, a very short moment, his eyes strayed to his sister; now with her back to him, with a shawl wrapped around her shoulders. Looking so pathetic and helpless again. As she usually did. And he was confused. So very confused as to his feelings towards her. For only seconds before she had seemed a real woman to him. But those thoughts were brushed aside as Jacob stumbled in and crashed into the table. Giles picked up his books, stuffed them into his satchel, and hung it behind the door out of harms way.

"Where is he?" bellowed Jacob, taking a slug of beer from a stone flagon resting on his arm, steadying himself as he did so against the table.

"Where is he?" he shouted again, staring round the room with eyes oblivious to their surroundings.

"Where's who?" asked Giles, moving across the room so that Jacob was looking at him and not their sister.

"Your father, of course. Your bloody father. Where is he?"

His speech was slurred, but the two younger members of the family were used to that. It was a way of everyday life. Jenny was about to reply, but Giles held a finger to his lips and looked in her direction.

"He's not come home yet," he said, trying to show he was not afraid.

Jenny remained silent, holding the bottle of lamb's milk tightly to her breast.

"I can see that," screamed Jacob.

"I know he's not here. That's why I've had to walk all the bloody way from The Nags Head in this bloody snow."

He took another slug of beer.

"He never picked me up like he promised. He left me there to find my own way home. I'm freezing, I tell you. I'm bloody freezing. The bastard. The bloody bastard. I'll kill him when I see him"

The youngsters had seen their older brother annoyed and drunk before. Really annoyed. But never as bad as this. His eyes were red and rolling with anger, he was screaming like a banshee, and they had no idea what he was about to do next. Fortunately, where he had consumed so much alcohol, there was a distinct lack of coordination between his brain and his limbs. H e was desperately trying to reach Giles to drag the truth from him. For he still thought he knew where their father was. But the arms would not leave the table and the right leg would not move into a position where it would be in front of the left.

"C'm here, you little sod," he swore, waving the flagon of beer above his head. "C'm here where I can see you."

Giles was trying to make signs to Jenny; to leave them while she was still safe. To go upstairs. But she would have none of it. She was worried for Giles's safety. And the lambs too. They had woken with all the commotion, and were bleating for their foster mother. To them, that was the young girl holding their bottle of milk to her breast.

With one almighty surge, Jacob lunged forward towards Giles. With arms waving around his head like a windmill, legs wobbling from side to side beneath his body, he staggered across the room for a short distance. Then he lost his grip on the flagon, which sailed through the air above his head, and like a man leaping from a cliff, his limbs seemed to spread eagle as he lost all sense of balance. Crashing to the ground, a mighty gush came rushing from his lips as all the wind was knocked from his body. The flagon, as if in slow motion, dropped slowly to the ground, smashed into smithereens on the brown tiled floor and the contents ran like a newly formed lake around Jacob's head. Before his mind folded into complete oblivion he stared up at Giles with sightless eye, chuckled and said, "Look what I just done."

And then he was still.

# EIGHT

Garnett had good reason for not picking Jacob up from the Nags Head. He was drunk. It was as simple as that. Not as drunk as Jacob, maybe. But still drunk enough that he should not have been driving. Like so many of his mates from the Bull Inn. But then no one was going to stop him. Not with his reputation. The sober customers only saw him lurch out of the door and down the main steps. No one saw him stagger through the snow and on into Market Place, where he had parked the old Austin pick up earlier during the day.

As he approached, cursing as he so often did with a belly full of ale, Dog pricked up his ears and was the only living soul that saw him that night in amongst the cattle pens. A lesser animal would have been frozen stiff by now. But Dog had a strong constitution as well as a strong character. A few snowfalls during the day and a crisp wind to follow at night would do him no harm. Leaning over the edge of the pick up he watched silently as his adopted master leant against one of the empty pens, unbuttoned his trousers and urinated on the freshly fallen snow.

"Ah, my boy," he laughed aloud. "That's better. I been needing that for a long while. Never thought I would make it though."

Dog remained silent as his master buttoned up his trousers, staggered towards the truck, fell over twice, and finally clambered into the driver's seat. After a great deal of cussing and swearing he finally produced the key from one of his pockets and fumbled as he tried to guide it into its slot under the dash board. Eventually the task was complete and the old truck fired into life. Dog was thrown across the back of the truck as they bounced along out of the car park and onto the High Street. Luckily the rope which Garnett had secured him with earlier held fast, and being a sensible type of dog, he settled down amongst the hessian bags and loose straw that gave him some protection from the howling wind.

The time was late. For Garnett had been supping well into the night with his friends in The Bull. They had bought him rounds, and didn't he have to reciprocate. But now, with lights barely showing a few yards in front, and a fresh flurry of snow blowing like little darts before his eyes, he was hard pushed to keep to the road. Through the town of Fairford was not too bad. There were the houses lining the side of the main street to guide him. But once out onto the Lechlade road was another story. With side banks falling away into neighbouring fields, and a continual build up of snow where only the occasional car had passed by, Garnett needed all his skills as a motorist to keep the little pick up on a course that was straight and true.

As he reached a bend in the road, no more than two miles out of Fairford and maybe three from Lechlade, the inevitable happened. Garnett, squinting through the windscreen, as the wipers struggled to keep it clear, saw the right hand bend just a little too late. By the time he had reacted to the situation and pulled hard over to the right, the wheels were already locked into a narrow ditch running along the left hand side of the road. Pulling even harder on the steering wheel, he tried to pull out of the ditch, but as the front wheel hit the roots of a tree, the truck bounced down a steep bank and came to rest in a pile of snow in a farmer's field. Garnett received a sharp bang to the head, which rendered him unconscious and Dog, in the back of the truck, was thrown out, only to be snatched back again as the rope drew taught, nearly throttling him and leaving him gasping for breath as he lay motionless alongside his master's door.

## NINE

Time was getting on when Chas Hanks pulled his cattle lorry into Holly Bank farm with the three in calf heifers aboard. They were his last drop off for the night and he would be glad to unload them and get off home to his bed. The falling snow was already piling up around the gateway, and rather than risk his lorry getting stuck in a drift, he tooted the horn. Giles was the first to look out through the iced up window, followed by Jenny, who hadn't long settled her lambs down for the night.

"Who is it?" She asked, pushing her body up against his to get a better view.

"Can't tell from here" said Giles, aware of her female scent that seemed far more prolific now than it used to be. Maybe he was more aware of it now that he was older. But whatever the reason, he knew he liked it. And that alone made him feel slightly awkward.

Pulling away from the window he said "I'd better go and take a look," as he stepped over the spread eagled body of his brother Jacob, still laying on the floor.

"You be careful," said Jenny, still peering through the window. "It could be anyone at this time of night."

"Don't you fret about me," smiled Giles, taking a long, thick hawthorn stick from behind the back door; the one his father used for herding the cattle.

"If they take a swipe at me they'll have this to put up with."

Jenny smiled as he left the room. She was so proud of him, the way he carried out his studies and how he always made out he was old enough to protect her, no matter what the situation was that arose.

It wasn't long before he returned. Chas followed, stamping the snow from his boots onto the door mat and closing the door behind him.

"It's Chas," said Giles, walking to the table as Jenny turned to face them. "You know, Chas Hanks from Lechlade. He owns the cattle lorry."

Jenny nodded and gave the merest hint of a smile. She didn't know Chas that well, and anything more could well have been construed as being a bit forward.

"That's right," said Chas, removing his cap and standing with his hands clasped in front of him. "Your Dad bought three in calf heifers at Fairford market today and asked me to deliver them home."

He paused as he stared at Jacob snoring on the floor, then he resumed.

"I would have been here sooner, but for the snow. The roads have got pretty bad in places. I won't be sorry to unload and be on my way home."

"Won't you stay and have a mug of tea when you've unloaded?" Asked Jenny, being polite and sociable. "It'll warm you up for the journey home. And it'll be no trouble, the kettle's already warm."

Chas shook his head.

"Best not, thanks. It'll take me a while to get back home. And me mum always worries if I'm back too late."

Glancing down at Jacob he added "Looks like you could do with a hand with him though. Reckon he ought to be in bed, didn't he?"

Jenny smiled awkwardly.

"It would be nice to have the place clear again. That's if you wouldn't mind."

"No trouble at all," he said, placing his cap in his pocket and scooping Jacob up off the floor like he weighed no more than a bag of feathers.

"You just show me the way, young'n, an' we'll have him up there in two shakes of a dog's tale."

Giles led the way up the stairs and into the bedroom he shared with Jacob while Jenny mopped up the spilt beer from the floor and cleared away the remains of the smashed flagon. As she waited for them to return she marveled at the strength of the young lorry driver. She guessed he was no more than twenty one or twenty two, but he handled Jacob in such a way that she had never seen before. That was when another germ of an idea formed in her mind as to how to leave the predicament she was in. With someone like Chas to take care of her, she would have nothing to fear. She guessed he would even be a match against her father. And there weren't too many men around you could say that about. Maybe ending up with Chas might not happen. After all, she didn't know him that well, but he did only live out at Lechlade. And that was just up the road. She smiled and the thought gave her hope.

The man and the boy came back down the stairs and Chas said "We've taken his boots off so he doesn't dirty the bed. He'll sleep best part of the night, I reckon."

Jenny thought how considerate. Removing Jacob's boots. Not too many men she knew would have even thought of doing that.

"Young Giles here tells me he had a skin full today," he added, walking to the door and replacing his cap.

Jenny smiled and said "It looked that way, yes."

"Not to worry," he said with a cheeky grin.

"We've all done it in the past."

Jenny smiled. And he noticed.

"Lads, I mean." He said awkwardly.

"Lads. I don't mean ladies like yourself."

Jenny felt her cheeks begin to glow. She had never been called a lady before. And by such a handsome young lad as well. With his long jet black hair, and the blue eyes, that caught flickering strands of light coming from the parlour lamp, set off in the corner of the room.

"Well," he said to Giles, who was leaning against the door," We'd best get these tykes unloaded before your dad comes home. He'll be none too pleased if they're not bedded down for the night, and that's for sure."

Jenny interrupted before he opened the door.

"I was just wondering, Chas. Did you see anything of our dad on your way through from Fairford tonight? Only it seems a bit late for him to still be out in this weather."

Chas shook his head.

"Can't say as I did. Only that doesn't mean a thing. He could have holed up for the night with a friend, or someone he met up with. What with the roads being so treacherous and all. Last time I saw him was late this afternoon at auction, when he asked me to bring the cattle home."

She nodded.

"Oh well," she said. "Maybe he'll arrive back soon."

"Aye, I expect your right," he agreed.

As he walked through the door followed by Giles, he turned back and said with a twinkle in his eye "I may as well take you up on that offer of a mug of tea. That's if the offer's still open."

Jenny could barely contain her excitement.

"Of course it is," she said with a broad smile.

"I'll warm it up straight away."

As she returned to the range there was a definite spring to her gait that wasn't there before.

## TEN

As the night wore on, Garnett lapsed in and out of consciousness a number of times. Whether it was the cold of the night air, added to by the falling snow, or the severe pains in his arms and head that caused it was hard to know. Strange though, there was no pain in his legs. Yet he knew they were trapped amongst the twisted metal behind the engine. But there was no feeling in them at all; or his back. Any lesser man would have long been dead. But for all his faults, Garnett was a survivor. And he swore to himself, during the times when he was conscious, that the good Lord was not about to take him yet.

Struggling to open the door from his position in the up turned pick up he cursed when he was unable to force the handle.  Where the doors were buckled, so the handles were jammed. He knew he had to make a decision. If he remained as he was, with the doors and windows shut, he would stand more chance of surviving against the elements, but there was also the question as to whether anyone would find him 'till the snow cleared, and that could be days away. On the other hand, if he could smash a window, if Dog was still alive, if he could free him from the rope, and if the stupid old bugger was in good enough shape to make his way home and raise the alarm; and if on top of all that the family could find him before he perished as the wind howled through the broken window, as it surely would, then he might stand a better chance of survival. But there seemed to be one hell of a lot of ifs to contend with and little else.

As he was thinking of all these ifs he lapsed into unconsciousness again. It was more than an hour before he came too, and he was just about lucid enough to know he had to make a decision one way or the other, and make it fast. He remembered the wrench he always carried in the truck. He had used it on a number of occasions. Some to defend himself; others to carry out summary justice on those who disagreed with him. Searching the darkness in the truck, spasmodically lit by the moon as it glowed through gaps in passing clouds, he felt something cold and hard near his feet. Clutching hold with his one free hand, and ignoring the pain that ripped through his arm, he slowly pulled the wrench from its resting place and smashed the window with one mighty blow that took away most of his strength. With the glass shattered, the howling wind rushed through into the cab, piercing needles of ice stabbing at his flesh. Despite the agony, he reached out, desperate for any sign of Dog. The feel of his coat, the cold black nose, the rope that held him. Anything. But if he did feel anything, then he was well past that state where nerve endings in the fingers can differentiate between hair, flesh, rope or snow. Garnett's senses were fading fast, and he knew it.

When he came too again, some time later, snow had already covered his arm and was creeping into the cab. It felt heavy and lifeless when he tried to move. His left arm was trapped somewhere behind him. Using every muscle in his shoulder he somehow managed to flick his arm like a whip and as if in a dream, although he was sure there was no more movement from his arm, the snow was slowly parting. A gap in the fleeting clouds allowed light to shine down from the moon. He felt strange. Like he was no longer in the real world. Maybe that was it. Maybe he was leaving this world and moving into the next. There to meet his maker. God, he hoped not. He had so much more he wanted to do with his life. Surely he wasn't going to be taken like this. All alone. Apart from a stupid old dog.

That was it. Suddenly it was becoming clearer now. Like a ghostly form in the cold blue grey of the night he could just about make out a dog's muzzle showing through the snow. A black muzzle with a dark grey face. Half an ear on one side , an eerie wall eye on the other; staring up at him. It was Dog. It just had to be Dog. And he was alive. The wall eye was moving as he blinked in the night. He knew he was alive now. Only trouble was though, thought Garnett, the stupid dumb animal was laying across his arm making it impossible for him to move. For a while both man and animal stared at each other. Both in pain. Both with very different feelings. The man was desperate for the dog to move. To free his arm so he could further plan his rescue. The poor old dog, on the other hand, was quite happy to lay where he was and freeze to death. But did that matter. He was with his master. That was the most important thing in his life right now.

Summoning all his strength, Garnett cursed at the animal, and shouted "Home."

The dog, ignoring the command, wriggled through the snow towards his master, and began to lick his face, sensing that would help him to survive. This small movement was enough to free Garnett's arm. Pulling it sideways, with the wrench still held firmly in his hand, he raised his arm and brought the wrench firmly down on Dog's back with a sharp crack. The poor old creature yelped in pain and leapt up into the air.

"Home" yelled Garnett, with the last of his strength ebbing fast. "Home you bugger, 'afore I kill you."

Fortunately for Garnett he had never used a tight collar on Dog, and as the animal leapt into the air and pulled away from the truck, so the collar slipped up his neck and over his head, freeing him and allowing him to scramble up the bank and onto the main road. What happened to him after that Garnett was not sure, for he slowly drifted into unconsciousness once again.

ELEVEN

Jenny, Chas and Giles were seated around the old pine kitchen table, nearly finished with their mugs of tea. Chas had been really good company for the past half hour, and Jenny would be sorry to see him go. He was a lad full of confidence, ready with a joke, even if one or two were a bit smutty, and he made her feel comfortable. Giles seemed to like him too, even though Chas wasn't that bothered about traveling around the world to see other lands belonging to the British Empire. Places like Africa, India and Canada. In fact, most of the places he'd never heard of. He was more than happy settled here in the Cotswolds, and he had no intentions of going traveling any farther than maybe Oxford to the South and Northampton to the North. That would do him, and let others go farther afield if they wished.

As the three of them sat round talking and joking, with Jacob snoring his head off upstairs, there came a scratching at the back door.

"What on earth can that be?" asked Jenny, jumping up from her chair.

"And at this time of night."

Looking at the old wooden clock ticking away above the fireplace she saw that it was getting on towards eleven o'clock.

"Don't worry," said Chas, standing up and placing himself subconsciously between her and the door as a form of protection.

"I'll take a look if you like. I'll see it'll do you no harm."

How different he was to her brother and father, she thought. If only she were married to a man like him.

Slowly, but with a great air of confidence, he walked towards the door and lifted the latch. Pulling the door towards him he was most surprised to see Dog limp in, cross the floor and lay down by the range, taking no notice at all of the two lambs fast asleep in their cardboard box.

"Whose dog is that, then?" he asked, closing the door to keep the draft out and walking back across the room to lay his hands upon the animal's back.

"That's Dog. He belongs to our Dad," said Giles, who sensed there was something seriously wrong.

Kneeling down, Chas talked quietly to Dog, moving large rough hands softly over his body.

"This old feller's in a bad way," he said gently stroking the animal's head.

"He's been out in that weather for some time and I reckon he's had a knock or two. If you ask me, he'll be lucky to make it through the night."

Jenny had never taken to Dog. She had great respect for him though; he had nipped her once or twice. But she would never have wished him any harm.

She looked towards Giles.

"There must be something wrong. He would never leave Dad normally. He's always with him You know that."

What a change in Giles. Earlier that evening he had seemed almost a young man. Living on his dreams. Explaining to Jenny how easy it would be to leave. To run away together. But now, with the awful truth staring him in the face, that his father may be out there somewhere in this awful blizzard, for blizzard it had become. Now, with real life staring him in the face, he was at a loss what to do. He just stared down at Dog and said nothing.

Chas stood up and turned to Jenny.

"We'll have to go out and look for your Dad. You and me. We'll leave Giles here in case he returns. And in case Jacob comes down; and wonders what's going on."

Jenny nodded. Pleased for someone to be making decisions. Not that she really wanted to find her Dad. Whenever he was around she was never easy in herself. But he was still her father. And like they say, blood is thicker than water.

"I'll find a blanket," she said. "To cover Dog."

"And you'd best bring two or three more along with you in case we find him. He'll need some keeping warm on a night like this." said Chas

Jenny nodded and ran up stairs.

"A bad night, is this," said Chas, "and that's for sure."

Giles nodded and stared down at Dog. What an ugly creature he was. And he smelt.

"Does your Dad keep any whisky about the place," asked Chas, breaking into he young lad's thoughts.

Giles thought for a moment. The he remembered. Walking over to the Welsh dresser he pulled a bottle, three quarters full, from behind one of the blue and white plates lined regimentally in three rows along the top section. His mother had been a great collector of plates, especially the old spode blue and whites, whenever she could afford them.

Handing the bottle to Chas he said "I shan't tell my Dad you had some."

As an afterthought he added "If you find him."

Chas looked surprised for a moment then chuckled.

"This isn't for me, you young fool. It's for you Dad. It might be just what he needs if we're to keep him alive."

Giles smiled awkwardly, nodded and was relieved as Jenny ran down the stairs into the room.

"Here," she said, handing all but one to Chas. "Will this be enough?"

"That'll do fine," replied Chas, throwing them under his arm, and placing his cap on top of his head.

"And now we'd best get going if we're to find him."

Jenny knelt down and covered Dog with the spare blanket. It was as much as he could do to look up at her, but he made the effort and seemed to be showing he was grateful. As he lowered his head there were tears in Jenny's eyes, and she patted his head gently with her soft white hands.

"You take care of him," she said to Giles. "And if we're not back within a couple of hours you feed the lambs if they wake up."

"How do I do that?" asked the young lad. "I've never done it before."

"But you've seen me do it enough times," said Jenny, almost a little annoyed. "Just make sure the milks not too hot. Try a drop on the back of your wrist. If it feels lukewarm it should be all right."

Looking into his eyes, she gave her young brother a hug, and told him to wish them luck. Then she was away, following Chas, out into the raging blizzard. Giles closed the door behind him, and he was all alone.

# TWELVE

Jenny climbed in to the cab of the lorry and slammed the door shut.

"You all right?" asked Chas, turning the key, and waiting for the engine to fire into life.

"If you're cold you want to throw a few of these blankets around you."

Jenny took them from Chas and did as he suggested. With the wind howling and temperatures below zero, she knew she would have to do her best to stay warm if she was to help in the recovery of her father.

Giving the engine a minute or so to warm up, Chas turned on the lights, slammed the gear lever into reverse and backed slowly away from the gate way.

"Be careful behind," said Jenny, "there's a deep ditch on the other side."

Chas heeded her warning

"We don't want to end up in there," he laughed. "Not before we even get started..."

The moon was giving off a cool clear glow and he caught sight of Jenny's face inside the cab. Chas thought how soft and kind she looked. He also noticed the bruises on her lips. He'd not wanted to say anything earlier, for fear of causing any embarrassment in front of her brother. But now, pushing the lever into first and guiding the lorry away from the gateway and out onto the road, he decided to ask her the cause.

Pulling the lever into second gear he said "Hope you don't mind me asking you Jenny, but your lips look like they've taken a bit of a bashing some time recently. How did that happen?"

He didn't see the look in her eyes as she turned to face him, for he was staring out at the lie of the road. Searching desperately for the banks either side that merged with the white and blue all around them. Jenny stared back at the road as well, lest he should turn and face her.

"One of the milking cows flicked me hard with her tale this morning," she said, with very little conviction in her voice. And Chas sensed this too. But he said nothing, save "Oh, right. I see."

He sensed there was a far graver situation than an old cow flicking her tale to cause such injuries; and he had noticed the dried cuts and bruises to her hands when she handed him the blankets. But he was a sensitive lad. Not likely to cause embarrassment to other people if he could help it. Besides which, if Jenny had a liking to tell him the truth at a later date, then no doubt she would. As for now though, he would keep his counsel. But he was still wondering if her father or brother Jacob had something to do with it as he negotiated the first bend of the road between Buscot and Lechlade. Easing on the steering wheel he remembered the time two years back when he kicked his step father out of the family home for laying a hand too many on his mother. That man was of similar stature to Jenny's father, but he never took up the offer to try and return home again. Even though Chas suggested he might like to try.

# THIRTEEN

Giles was all alone. He was trying to read his books on the British
Commonwealth, of places far away. Of places he dreamed of. Where he could
forget the life he lead now; of the hardship, of the boredom, of the farming life.
But this was proving too much. What with a dog that kept grunting and
groaning in pain, two lambs that kept shifting in their sleep, the howling wind
outside and odd branches crashing into the side of the house as they were torn
apart from their parent trees. That was bad enough. But the incessant snoring of
his brother Jacob upstairs was more than he could bear.

He should have been used to it, he knew that. For they shared the same small,
cramped bedroom each night. But often, if he was lucky enough, he would be in
bed and asleep before Jacob climbed the stairs to join him. Now though, the
worry was that every time there was a pause in Jacob's snoring there was the
fear he may be waking up from his slumber and coming downstairs, where
Giles would have to explain away what had occurred that night. Not that
anything untoward had happened. Only that their father may be lying in a snow
drift somewhere on the road between here and Fairford, breathing his last. The
family dog, for he could not in truth call it a pet, was on its last legs. And
finally, a virtual stranger by the name of Chas Hanks, had spent a fair bit of the
evening in their house and now gone off with their sister in a cattle lorry with a

bottle of whisky belonging to their dad. No, there wasn't too much to worry about. He was sure Jacob would take it all in his stride.

## FOURTEEN

The journey to Lechlade took them twenty minutes. It should have taken them no more than five or six. But the roads were atrocious, although the blizzard had spent itself out, and Chas was well pleased when he pulled into the town up alongside the Police House.

"You wait here," he shouted, as he climbed down from the lorry and slammed the door shut. "I shan't be long."

Jenny was more than happy to remain where she was. She shivered slightly as she watched him walk towards the freshly painted royal blue front door, now partially covered with streaks of snow. The more she knew Chas the more she liked him. And he was strong and powerful as well. It also appeared he had no fear of the Law. Not like her father; who had no respect for it whatsoever. And sure, wasn't it Chas who suggested they call into the local constabulary and ask for assistance. After all, they had narrowed the search down somewhat. They were pretty sure her dad wasn't on the Buscot to Lechlade road; or as sure as any soul could be on a night like this. That only left the road to Fairford; if their thinking was right it was the route he would have taken home.

The constable on duty was not over impressed to receive customers at this late hour. He eyed Chas up for a few moments; but said nothing. He was a stalwart man; some might say plump. His face had reddened with age and liquor; the moustache he supported was drooping on either end. The serge uniform appeared a trifle tight, even with the tunic buttons undone. Being half way through a kipper paste sandwich his wife had prepared for the night shift, he was not as over enthusiastic as Chas would have liked.

"A missing person, you say?"

Chas nodded.

The constable leant across the counter, pencil in hand; ready to make an entry in the day book.

"That's right," replied Chas. "A local farmer from round these parts."

"You might know him," he added as the officer turned to the current page.

"Oh aye, and who might that be?" he asked with pencil poised.

"Couling. Garnett Couling," replied Chas.

At the mention of the name the whole atmosphere changed. The officer held his pencil in mid air, raised his eyebrows and stared deep and hard into Chas's eyes. For a moment or two there was complete silence, save for the ticking of a wall clock set above the door leading into cells at the rear of the station.

"And what's he been up to this time?" he asked. "Got drunk, I wouldn't be surprised, and upset someone else along the way."

"No," said Chas, shaking his head and explaining as swiftly as he could what had happened. He knew time was of the essence if they were to save Jenny's father.

"And you're sure he's out there somewhere on the Fairford road?" asked the officer, scribbling a note in the day book for his colleagues to read when they returned from a domestic dispute he had sent them to earlier.

"As sure as we can be," replied Chas. "Like I say, we've checked as best we can along the road from here out to Buscot."

"And you're sure he couldn't be holed up with friends for the night, 'till the weather improves?" he asked, buttoning his tunic. As he reached for his cape, hanging on a hook above the door, he looked quizzically at Chas for a moment, then shook his head.

" 'course not. Damn stupid question really. No one would ever put up with him, would they?"

Chas smiled, as it was probably true, and made his way back to his lorry; followed by the older man after he had turned out the light and securely locked the big heavy oak door that marked the entrance to the Police station.

"Evening miss," he said, climbing inside the cab, hissing and wheezing, leaving very little room for Jenny as they shared the single seat.

"Don't you fret none," he added, slamming the door too and struggling to get himself comfortable. "We'll soon find your dad. Have no fear of that."

Jenny nodded and said thank you. With hands clasped tightly in her lap, she once more turned to stare out of the window, eager to be on their way.

# FIFTEEN

Pain is a terrible thing, and so it was for Garnett, laying out there all alone, in the ice and the snow. Not even his grey old dog to keep him company. Waves of pain had been sweeping in and out like tides being pulled by the moon. As they brought him back to consciousness, so he willed them to release him from his torment. To end this nightmare now. To let him die. Out here, all alone. Just once more, allow him to lapse back into unconsciousness, to let this be an end to it all. Never having to face such pain again.

He tried in vain to concentrate on his legs, where there seemed to be an empty void. A nothingness. A place where he could go and feel safe, and warm. Where he could escape the cold and the heat. The snow and the pain. But whoever controls such things, whether it be the Lord up above or the Devil down below, they were having none of it. This was where he was, and this was where he would stay. In agony he tried to scream out loud. To release some of the tension that held his body taught. To let him relax. But no sound came. Just a small hiss that he barely recognized having come from his own mouth.

The hiss was similar to the sound he could hear in the distance. Or thought he could hear. Way, way off. Maybe there, maybe not. Maybe the sound came from his mind. He was not sure. But if it was for real then he was sure it was drawing closer. Forcing himself harder now, to climb that steep slope back up to the here and now, he suffered even more pain. And he swore to himself, for he could not swear aloud. How easy it would have been now to slip back into that nothingness. The way he had wanted to before. But now he had to stay awake, if he were to survive.

Nearer and nearer drew the hissing sound. He part recognized it. It was similar to a sound he knew so well. But he still could not place it. Not by the sound. And so he began to use his eyes.

# SIXTEEN

Three times Chas had stopped the lorry. Three times they had climbed out, slid down a bank of virgin snow, searched in vain because one of them thought they had heard a sound, or seen a light. And now, as they returned once more to the cab, the constable cursed under his breath. Did he really need this? On one of the coldest nights yet in the winter of 1928. To be out here, searching for a man he did not like. Just so he could say he had done his duty. Who was the fool, he wondered.

Jenny waited until he climbed in and pulled the door shut before she pulled her shawl and the blankets around her. If she had been colder than this, she could not remember when. If the windows had been shut, at least the inside of the cab would have been warmer than the weather outside. But they needed them open. To hear even the slightest sound could raise their hopes. Well, maybe not the constable's. But hers, and maybe those of Chas.

And so they continued, along the road between Lechlade and Fairford. And now, with little more than two miles to Fairford, the chances of finding Garnett alive were growing slim.

## SEVENTEEN

As Garnett watched the lights approaching, more like a zombie from the grave than a human being, he felt sure they were growing larger. What that meant he was not sure. Think, man. Think. If something grows larger, what does it mean. His mind, searching desperately for an answer, was already sinking back into that beautiful land where pain is no more.

Suddenly, and without warning, like a bolt from the blue, it came to him. What made him remember he didn't know. Maybe it was the extra surge of pain as he tried to ease himself up onto one elbow. But it was enough. Just enough to combine the two. The lights and the hissing sound. The two, merged together could only mean one thing. A motor vehicle. A truck, a car, a lorry. Whatever.

But if it was moving, then logic told him there had to be people inside. And people meant help. If only he could hold on long enough for them to reach him. But the more his brain became alert, as new hope forced him out of that land where pain is no more, so he began to realize that the people, whoever they may be, might not see him. Down here, at the bottom of the bank. He must do something, before they pass.

The lights of the approaching vehicle had shown him something. That something was out there. A vehicle with people. But it was the light that had shown him they were there. And that was where the answer lay. If he could see them, then he must make sure they could see him. Before they pass him by. He must somehow let them see. But how? What had he got, out here in the darkness, that would show them the way? For what seemed an eternity he thought long and hard. And only when his brain ached and his mind was almost gone did it come to him. The lights of his own pick up. Turn them on. They would light up his position. They would be the beacon in the night. But as his brain cleared so he realised they were already on. Or had been. When the pick up rolled down the bank. But that was hours ago. Now they were dead. No light at all. Gone. The battery. Of course. The battery would be dead. So the lights would be dead.

He had to think fast. He must do something. If only Dog had been here. He could have barked, yelped. Anything. To have raised the alarm. But Dog had long gone and left him. When he brought the wrench down on his back and sent him home. The wrench. Of course. That was it. Was it still in his hand? That was difficult to tell for there was no life in his arm. The snow, now piled up high against the cab of the truck had frozen it long ago. But somehow he managed to wriggle his fingers and felt something hard within his grasp. It had to be the wrench. It couldn't be anything else. Even with his mind about to slip back into oblivion, he seemed to know the wrench was there.

Gathering the last of his strength before it ebbed away; he brought the wrench up and struck it hard against the side of the cab. The resounding crash brought

even more pain as the vibrations seemed to reverberate around inside his head.

But he continued to beat the side of the cab with all his might until he could do

no more.

## EIGHTEEN

Jenny Couling found her father's body that night. Stiff and cold, like a corpse. Colder than a corpse. A corpse has a mean temperature, according to the temperature around it. Her father's body was colder than that. Far colder.

Chas was the first to hear the clank of metal against metal. At first he thought it was his imagination; caused through the intense cold that seemed to seep into his brain with the window down. But when he heard it again, he stopped the engine and all three of them listened. A few more thuds and all was quiet. But it had been enough. They found him, still and lifeless, in the cab of his truck, in the field. Using one of the cattle dividing gates from the lorry as a stretcher Chas and the constable carried him back up the slope and placed his body in the back of the wagon.

"You'd best get going as fast as you can for the hospital, lad," and said the constable to Chas. "Me and the lass'l do what we can back here."

Nodding, Chas quickly bolted up the back of his lorry and climbed into the cab. Although the blizzard had ceased and no more snow was falling, the roads were still treacherous. No time for taking any chances.

Jenny and her companion wrapped blankets around Garnett and rubbed his body to restart any circulation that may have been there. There was the hint of a heart beat, but little else. The constable, in his wisdom, decided it best not to attempt to pour any of the whisky Chas had brought down into Garnett's throat. At least, not until he was conscious. Jenny agreed. However, due to the cold of the night, the constable did feel that a dram or two may help him survive the night. And Jenny was quite ready to agree.

"Do you think he'll pull through?" she asked, still rubbing her father's arms and chest as she looked down at him through the dim light from the old constabulary torch.

"He's got as much chance as any man I know," said the constable, enjoying the whisky, and even more so when he thought it belonged to Garnett Couling.

"He's a big man, and from my experience, the bigger they are, the better chance they have."

Jenny felt some comfort in his remark, but not much. And she had such mixed feeling about her dad. At times she was scared of him, at times she hated him. At times she liked him a little, and at times she loved him a lot. And maybe this was one of those times. She wasn't sure. Until, that is, he opened his eyes very slowly, there in the back of that cattle truck, surrounded by hay and straw that was meant for the cattle, looked up at his daughter and said in a weak, quiet voice "I'm sorry, lass. Forgive me."

And then he was gone.

# NINETEEN

Jenny arrived home in the early hours of the morning, accompanied by Chas. When they entered the parlour, Giles, Dog and the lambs were all asleep. Or appeared to be. Giles was leant forward across the table, his head resting on an open book. Dog was laying much the same as Jenny had left him, and the lambs were in their usual position, straddled across each other.

Jenny looked at Chas as he looked at her, and they nodded. Chas removed his cap and stood with his hand clasped in front of him, as he so often did. Slowly, and with tears in her eyes, Jenny crossed the parlour and placed an arm round Giles's shoulders. Sleepily he opened his eyes and looked up at her.

"Hello Jen," he said with a yawn and lowered his head back down again onto the book.

Jenny shook him gently.

"Giles," she said. "You've got to wake up. There's something I've got to tell you."

Again he opened his eyes.

"Are you awake?" She asked.

"I am now," he said with another yawn, almost as large as the first.

"We've found Dad," she said, lowering herself into the chair next to his.

"That's good then," he said, staring at her indifferently.

"No, it's not good. Not really," she said.

"Why?" he asked, now fully awake.

"Because it's bad news," she said.

For what seemed a long time to the pair of them they stared at each other. Giles was the first to speak.

"He's not dead, is he?"

"Not far off," she said, with tears in her eyes. "It's touch and go whether he'll make it through the night. That's why Chas and I have come back for you. We've had a word with the doctor. He thinks the family should be there; you know, just in case."

Giles stared vacantly towards the fire. Like Jenny, he hated his father at times; at times he loathed him. But when faced with a situation like this, not much else mattered.

"I'll get my coat," he said, leaving the table and walking sleepily towards the door.

"What about them?" he asked as an afterthought, nodding towards the two pet lambs and Dog.

"We'll have to leave them," replied Jenny. "And just hope they all behave themselves."

"And what about Jacob." asked Giles, thanking Chas, who gave him a hand to pull the jacket over his shoulders.

Jenny looked at Chas.

"I think we'll leave him, don't you," she said. "He's snoring loud enough to wake the dead. And he could well be trouble in the hospital"

Chas nodded.

"I can't see him coming round before morning anyhow. And we should be back by then."

Dog looked up and stared at Jenny as they began to leave. It was as though he sensed something was wrong, even though he was so weak. Then he lowered himself once more against the warmth of the grate and gave a groan.

## TWENTY

Hospitals. How Jenny hated hospitals. Especially Fairford hospital. The strong stench of antiseptic hanging heavy through the corridors and the wards. The unmistakable smell of carbolic soap, guaranteed to kill or clear every bug known to man. Row upon row of metal beds, each occupied by a man or a woman, a patient suffering. They watched and wondered, the three of them, as they passed, accompanied by the doctor in charge of the case. And the night nurses. The only saving grace in such places, with their starched white bonnets and aprons. God's angels in places of pain, misery and despair. And occasionally, hope. Yes, hope. Very little. Sometimes barely a spark. But always there, in the darkness. In a whisper, a sign, or maybe a smile. Always there for someone to grasp, if they had a mind to.

"This way," said the doctor, a man of middle years, with a spreading girth, grey hair and a genuine smile.

"We had to move him to another room since you were last here. Another emergency came in."

Giles was more surprised than any of them. His father looked so frail, so weak, laying there on the bed, white blankets covering him, pipes and tubes twisting from various parts of his body. He had been such a big man. So strong, so powerful. Could he really change, in such a short space of time? Where was the colour. The redness in his cheeks. The ruggedness of his face. All replaced now with a pallor, greyness. So ghostly in the paleness of the night.

"Will he live?" Stammered Giles, half afraid to edge too close to his father, in case he caused him further injury.

"We can't be sure," replied the doctor sincerely, as he stood alongside the bed and measured Garnett's feeble pulse.

"He's very weak. We'll know more in twenty four hours."

Having read the notes from the board at the end of the bed he nodded to all three of them and, with a sympathetic smile, left the room. Chas remained near the door, allowing Jenny and Giles to move closer, one on either side of the bed. All three stared down at Garnett, all three with very different thoughts.

# TWENTY ONE

Morning had arrived early in the Cotswolds. A bright crisp morning, with plenty of sunshine and a coolness in the air. Jacob, however, was not one to rise early, unless he had to. But this morning he had; and probably wished he hadn't. His head was heavy and ached. His tongue was rough like sandpaper and it tasted foul. His eyes ached. He was not a happy man. Squinting in the sunlight he cursed aloud as he pulled on a pair of boots that had been removed by Chas the night before. Not that he remembered much about last night. It was more a haze, that turned into nothingness. A feeling that he had grown accustomed to, but never used to.

Inching his way down the stairs, careful not to jar his aching head, the door into the parlour was finally reached. Crossing the room and pulling the curtains apart, allowing the morning light to enter, he turned and stared down at the twin pet lambs and Dog. Trying to understand why the dog was inside the house, and having no idea why it was there, he bellowed allowed.

"Jenny. Where are you?"

Dog woke from his slumber and turned to look up at Jacob.

"What're you looking at?" he snarled, forcing the dog to shy away.

"You shouldn't be in here, anyway."

"Jenny," he bellowed again. "Get down here right now, 'afore I come up there after you."

For a moment he stared at the empty pine table, unable to understand why a breakfast was not laid out before him it seemed strange. No answer from his sister. No sign of his father or brother; and a flea ridden mongrel laying on the hearth in front of him. Staggering back up the stairs he searched each room in turn, calling for each member of the family, waiting for a reply. But no answer came. Standing on the landing he looked first this way, then that, half expecting they were hiding away from him in some sort of game; thinking they might suddenly reappear. But there was no sign of them. It was like they had disappeared from the face of the earth. Like in that ship. The Mary Celeste. He had heard about that. Where it had been found. With all the crew missing. And yet, all the food laid out ready to be eaten. Except that in this household, there was no food; it had not been laid out. There was not even a crust of bread anywhere to be seen.

## TWENTY TWO

As Jacob was searching Holly Bank Farm for his family, so Jenny and Chas were preparing to leave Fairford Hospital. Garnett had survived the night, although he was still unconscious. But the duty doctor had said he was stable, and Jenny knew she had to face Jacob at some time to explain what had happened. Giles had pleaded with her to allow him to stay, and she could see the sense of it. If their father came too, it would make him feel easier to find one of the family there by his bed side.

During the night Chas had driven his lorry home, which was a neat little terrace house set in Lechlade town. His mother was worried as he was late home, but once he had explained, she settled down and was more than happy for him to help Jenny out for as long as it take. Satisfied she was well, he had returned to the hospital and offered his services for the rest of the day.

"What about your customers" Jenny had asked.

"Won't they be expecting you to do some deliveries?"

He shook his head.

"Nothing on very urgent today," he lied, thinking of Harry Dawson's herd of forty odd Hereford suckling cows that needed transferring to his new farm out Cirencester way over the next couple of days.

"Nothing that can't keep 'till tomorrow."

She thanked him and touched his arm with her rough, but dainty hand. They smiled at each other, and were becoming good friends, in just a short space of time.

The journey home was far less arduous than the night before. The sun, already a bright red ball on the distant horizon, was giving off a reddish hue to the surrounding countryside, and as they traveled East, jackdaws and crows screeched from the overhanging trees as they passed. Keeping to the few tracks visible in the road was far easier. The old lorry, that had covered many a mile and seen many a year, bounced this way and that, as smoke belched from its exhaust. But it did them proud, and they arrived at Holly Bank Farm in one piece, ready to face Jenny's older brother and tell him what had happened to his father.

Jenny steeled herself as she led Chas through the back door. She was not looking forward to this one little bit. Already her stomach felt like it was in a tight knot and her hands were clammy with sweat. Jacob looked up from the kitchen table where he was finishing a slice of bread and butter, along with a mug of tea. His eyes closed deep and narrow as he looked at them curiously.

"An' where the hell have you been, girl?" he snarled, directing his remark towards Jenny, but turning slowly towards Chas.

She took in a deep breath and, whilst remaining close to Chas near the open door, she said in almost a whisper "We've got some bad news for you, Jacob."

"I'll bet you have," he growled again. "Been out all night with him and got yourself pregnant, I shouldn't wonder."

Although she was a foot or two away from Chas, she could sense his body stiffen. And she knew it was in anger. She also knew he would quite happily wade in and knock the living daylights out of Jacob, if she did not stop him. He may have been a quiet peaceable man, but he would also stand up for anything that was not right.

As she stood between the two country boys, both hard as nails, and eager to show their strength, she said in barely more than a whisper "If that's what you want to think, Jacob, then so be it. But if you want to know the truth, then our Dad's laying in hospital over at Fairford seriously ill."

For what seemed an eternity there was silence in the room as Jacob tried to understand what she had said. His brain was still addled from the night before, and from drinking over many years. It took him a while for the truth to sink in so he knew what she was talking about.

"Ill in hospital," he repeated. "Why, what's up with him?"

He remained silent as she explained what had happened during the past twelve hours or so. Of the long search for Garnett along the country roads in a howling blizzard. Of the drive to Fairford in the back of Chas's cattle lorry. Of the return journey to pick up Giles. And how Giles was still there now, at his bedside, ready for when he regained consciousness, if he ever did. And all the while, as the tears welled up in Jacob's eyes, Jenny was crossing the room towards him. Chas, as always, stood politely at the door. But unlike most times when he entered a room, his brown mottled cap stayed on his head.

Jenny placed her hand gently upon Jacob's shoulder and in a strange way, felt sorry for him.

"He's pulled through the night," she whispered. "There's every chance he could pull through."

"And be paralyzed for the rest of his life," he snapped, having heard Jenny say there was still no feeling in his legs.

"We don't know that. Not yet," she said, trying to reassure him.

"Of course we bloody do," he roared, pulling himself up to his full height and hurling her across the room. Like a sack of potatoes she collided into Chas, who reacted far too slowly from the sudden tirade. The two were tangled in a heap on the tiled stone floor, and as they tried to free themselves, all arms and legs, Jacob was climbing over them and running out into the yard. Once there, he spotted the lorry. Climbing into the cab he found the keys which had been left by Chas who, like so many other country folk, believed that most people were honest and could be trusted. The engine roared into life and by the time Chas and Jenny had untangled themselves, it was roaring away down the road towards Lechlade and on towards Fairford. Together they stood, side by side, staring after it as it disappeared round the bend and out of sight. With his right hand, Chas snatched the old brown mottled cap from his head and threw it to the floor in disgust.

"He'd just better watch out when I catch up with him," he snarled, and for the first time since they met, Jenny realised that amongst all his other qualities, Chas had a temper just like anyone else.

## TWENTY THREE

Jenny made breakfast for herself and Chas. A good plate of bacon, eggs and onions, along with black and white pudding and bread. Added to that, a mug or two of hot tea. And they were ready to face the world again.

Both had a quick wash to freshen themselves, and whilst Chas made his way on foot to Buscot, Jenny saw to the milking of the cows and the feeding of the hens. The sheep were not her responsibility, apart from orphan lambs and the two indoors, but as she was alone, she tended them today. Three more had been born overnight, along with a set of twins, and one of the older ewes needed some assistance to deliver her single lamb. Jenny did not like the pigs. They smelt; and she thought it was man's job to look after them. But today, again, it was down to her, and a bucket of scraps, along with some mash would satisfy them. The twenty five store cattle housed in one end of the barn were never any problem. A good heap of hay and ground corn in their manger, followed by a fair sprinkling of straw bedding would keep them happy for the rest of the day.

Chas, meanwhile, having crunched through the hardening snow and ice on the country road, had reached Buscot and made his way to the Nags Head. There was crystallized snow hanging over the porch and around the windows, and he shivered slightly as he knocked on the door. As he waited he was aware that the winter sun did not hold the heat needed to warm up the surrounding country side. It would be a month or two yet before folk around here could rely on that and do away with some of their heating.

After a while the large oak door, now aged with black, creaked open and Zack's daughter, Tammy, showed herself.

"Sorry Chas, my dear," she whispered with pouting lips and a smile thrown in for good measure, "but we're not open yet. Not even for you."

Shoving his hands deeper into his pockets he said with a reciprocal smile "I'm not after a pint, Tammy. It's your Dad I've come to see."

Placing a finger against his lips, she gave a mock frown and a sideways flick of her head, allowing the long ringlets of raven black hair to fall to one side of her neck and settle about her shoulder.

"You are a disappointment to me," she laughed, opening the door wider to allow him through, and giving him a squeeze on the bum as he passed. He was used to this form of attention from Tammy. They had been friends from childhood, when Chas used to live in Buscot, and they still remained firm friends now. If Chas had a notion to make advances towards her now, then who knows? But he had never had the inclination. And many people who knew them both said that she was too much of a handful for him. And maybe they were right. Or maybe he felt safer in the house he shared with his mother.

Zack soon appeared from the cellar and gave him a warm greeting, before leading him to one of the settles alongside the bar. At sixty three years of age the rheumatics had finally caught up with the old man, and pleased for a rest, he lowered himself stiffly onto the wooden bench. Chas pulled up a spare chair, Tammy brought over three mugs of coffee, and it was only when Zack frowned in her direction that she gave that haughty smile of hers, ran her finger along the back of Chas's neck, and disappeared out the back to drink her coffee alone.

"I worry about that girl," grumbled Zack. "And she's never made a good mug of coffee for as long as I can remember," he added, placing his mug on the table having tasted a sample.

"I shouldn't worry about Tammy," replied Chas, thinking his mug wasn't too bad. "If anyone can take care of themselves, I reckon she can."

Zack nodded.

"Maybe. But a father can't help worrying about his daughter. You'll find that out when you take a wife and have a few of your own."

Chas smiled. He had no intention of starting a family. Not yet, anyhow. He was only twenty two and didn't want to get tied down just yet. He had a cattle transport business he was building up. Maybe only one lorry right now; and he had a way to go. But he would get there in the end. And when he did, and when he was ready to take a wife, he would be in a position to provide for her like his Dad had for his Mum. Before he died.

Pushing these thoughts to one side he turned to Zack, who was testing the coffee once again. He explained what had happened overnight; at least that which was relevant. And Zack listened intently, as he always did, and pulled slowly on his pipe.        When Chas was finished, Zack blew smoke across the bar and watched it drift upwards, adding more nicotine to the already dark brown stained ceiling.

"He's a bad 'un, is that," he finally said with some thought. "If you ask me he's going to end up in real trouble one day."

"You could be right there," agreed Chas, who was now ready to reach the main reason for why he had walked over two miles of cold, crisp frost hardened snow in the middle of winter to get here.

"Truth is, Zack," he said plainly, "I need transport. Now he's taken my lorry I've got no way of getting over to Fairford Hospital. Jenny needs to see her Dad. And I reckon I'm the only one around to help her out."

Zack chuckled.

"An' you could do with one of my two motors, I suppose?"

Chas hopefully looked at the old man in such a way that showed he was sincere. They'd known each other for a fair number of years, and as for favours, they were about even; although Zack may have been in a slightly stronger position out of the two.

"Can't say as you've ever let me down in the past when you've had reason to use one," he said, looking at the coffee mug, deciding whether to down another gulp.

"And I wont let you down this time," said Chas sincerely, offering his hand.

Zack shook his head. He had decided to risk the coffee.

"No need for that, son." He said, holding the mug to his lips. "If I can't trust you with one of me motors, then I don't reckon I can trust anyone."

Chas was mighty grateful, and told him so.

"Think nothing of it," he replied, poking the fire back into life. "You go out there behind the bar and ask our Tammy to give you the key for the Austin 7. It's in the yard out the back."

Chas thanked him heartily and found Tammy cleaning some glasses. She teased him for a while, holding the keys in her hand, high enough that he had to stretch for them. And more than once she pressed her body close enough that he could feel the firmness of her breasts. She had nice breasts, he thought; large and firm. He often noticed her cleavage too, the times when he called in for a pint and she leaned across the bar to whisper in his ear. They excited him. The perfume too, it was strong and evocative. She always wore it; so different from Jenny. Only once had he noticed Jenny wearing perfume; not as strong as perfume. Maybe it was what they called rose water. Made from the petals of roses. He wasn't sure. He remembered they had been at a village dance a year or two back. And because Jenny had been the wallflower, he felt sorry for her. He asked her to dance, and although at first she refused he had, with some persuasion, guided her onto the dance floor. Neither of them enjoyed the experience much; neither of them could dance that well. And he did not ask her again. But he often recalled the scent and it reminded him of Jenny.

So different from Tammy. She was more the vixen. The tease. Always ready for a laugh. A kiss and a cuddle from other boys in the village. But Chas knew it was never serious with them. And that was why he never took advantage. When he got with a girl he wanted one he could rely on. One he could trust. Not one that he would be watching every five minutes unless she decided to flirt with another lad. He would have none of that.

Finally he left Tammy in the bar and found the maroon Austin 7 car in a make shift garage, housed alongside a sporty little Morgan Aero Sports. Zack owned the pair of them, but the Morgan was more for Tammy's use. It was painted mainly green, with more than its fair share of chrome, and came with only three wheels, two at the front for steering and a trailing wheel at the rear. She would often be seen cruising along the country lanes in the summer, her long black hair streaming out in the slip stream, waving to neighbours as she passed them by. Chas had to smile and shake his head as he climbed into the little Austin car. She was a popular girl around these parts, of that there was no mistake. And maybe she would settle down one day with someone. But who knows. Only . time would tell.

## TWENTY FOUR

Chas pulled the little Austin 7 into a parking bay outside the Victoria Hospital in Fairford and, along with Jenny and the constable he had collected from Lechlade; they searched in vain for his lorry.

"No sign of it here, son," said the officer, climbing out of the rear seat. "Maybe he parked it down the road a ways."

Chas could not see the logic of that. Jacob was mad with the world when he stole the lorry, and he was probably just as mad now. He was resigned to the fact that it could be a while before he got his lorry back, and that was a fact.

When they arrived at Garnett's bed, very little had changed. His mighty frame still lay motionless beneath the white cotton blankets that covered him. Tubes still twisted and turned from various parts of his body, and still that awful stench of antiseptic clung to the air. Giles was now asleep in a wooden framed chair alongside his father and the two men left it to Jenny to wake him. As consciousness brought him back to reality he looked straight to his father. Grabbing Jenny's arm he said "Will he be all right?"

His sister shook her head.

"We just don't know. We'll have to wait and see."

As the two drew closer together a woman dressed a in nurses uniform walked in and asked to speak to Chas and the police officer alone. Jenny moved to follow, but the woman shook her head and said it wasn't necessary. She just needed a few more details. And no, her father had not yet regained consciousness, but there was nothing to concern herself about at this stage.

Leading the two men into an anti room the nurse, a middle aged woman with striking red hair, closed the door and offered them each a chair. It could have been construed more of an order than an invitation. It certainly defied any argument. Both men were in awe her of authority, and dressed in a dark blue uniform, they guessed her rank to be that of a matron.

"We have a problem," she said, folding her arms across a well endowed bosom, which matched in proportion to the rest of her body.

Both men remained silent.

"I expect calm, peace and quiet in my hospital for it to run efficiently" she said, before pausing a moment.

"This morning we had chaos."

Chas knew what was coming next and he looked at the officer, who nodded in agreement.

"The son of that patient lying in there," she continued, pointing towards the emergency department, "came roaring in here less than two hours ago like some raging wild bull. He caused pandemonium amongst my staff and fear amongst my patients." She paused just long enough for the seriousness of her remarks to have effect. "I'm not having it, do you hear. I am just not having it."

Both men remained silent for a while and it was the officer who spoke first.

"And quite right too, matron" he said when he knew Chas was going to remain silent, and hoping for the sake of his own safety that he had addressed her at the correct rank in the nursing profession. But he then went quiet and sat with his hands in his laps like a scorned school boy, waiting for a further reprimand.

"Well, what are you going to do about it?" asked the matron, staring down at them.

Now that was a very good question and neither really had the answer. And Chas did not want to get too involved anyway. He didn't mind a straight fight out in the open with Jacob, bare fists or whatever. But in a hospital was a different matter altogether. And after all, hadn't he handed the matter over to the Police.

"A lot depends, ma'am, on where he is," offered the constable.

"How do I know where he is?" she snapped. "I kicked him out of here shortly after he came in. He could be anywhere by now. It's your job to find him."

Both men could imagine Jacob being kicked from the hospital grounds by this woman; and at any other time they would have had a good laugh at his misfortune. But now was not really the time. And although the remark on finding him was directed at the constable, Chas also felt that he was duty bound to assist. Even if it meant leaving Jenny for a while.

"We'll get out there searching for him now'" said the older of the two men, taking it for granted that Chas would be helping him out.

"Of course we will," agreed Chas eager to escape the powers of this monstrous woman.

"And I should hope you would," she snapped, opening the door and allowing them an escape route to their freedom.

## TWENTY FIVE

As Chas and his companion left the hospital in search of a lorry thief, a young girl and her brother continued their silent vigil by the side of their father's bed. Occasionally there would be a movement, a twitch of the hand, a groan from the throat. But no other sign to show he was stirring from his deep subconscious dream. A nurse would enter occasionally to check his pulse and other vital signs; a doctor would visit and with a colleague, discuss his chart. But no one spoke to the children. And why should they. Although Jenny appeared to have matured and gained confidence over the past thirty six hours, with the trauma encapsulating her, she was still a child. Only four years senior to her twelve year old brother. No one would pay them much heed.

Chas had treated her more as an equal than any other adult she had known. Other than her mother. She had warmed to him and felt safe in his company, and it was only now, with him not at her side, and the lack of sleep during the previous night, that she felt very much alone; and a very vulnerable young girl.

As one hour slipped into another, and morning drifted into afternoon, she wondered, as she sat in a chair in the emergency room, what the future would hold. She'd heard from the matron that Jacob had been and gone earlier that morning and as of now she did not wish to think of him. But think of him she must. He was her elder brother. An integral part of her family. From spasmodic, often callous conversations with the doctors, she had learnt that her father may never walk again. Until tests had been carried out when he was conscious, it was impossible to say whether any serious injuries had been caused to his spinal column. And when Jenny asked what that meant they explained to her as simply as they could that it was his back bone.

If he were paralyzed, and there was every possibility that he may, then life on the farm would take on a very different meaning. There were very many ifs and buts involved. Would he be able to cope with life in a wheel chair; not able to carry out his farming or his beloved dealing. Would Jacob settle down and take to farm work without his father to chivy him along. To date he had only suffered life on the farm because he had to. Because, at the end of the day, you could say he was almost as scared of his father as Jenny was. But without the discipline of their father, crippled in a wheelchair, would Jacob take off and look for work elsewhere, and only return at night to sleep off a belly full of ale.

And what of Giles. His school days would soon be coming to an end. His ambition was already to leave the farm and travel. To see the world. And once away from the farm, Jenny believed he would have the confidence to do so. But again, with their father unable to leave his chair, and Jenny unable to carry out all the work, would Giles be required to stay on the farm to help out. And if so, what type of relationship would he and Jenny enjoy. Not, she guessed, as pleasant as it was now. She knew, only too well, the last thirty six hours would have a great impact on her young life. And as it unfolded, she would have to adapt accordingly.

At three o'clock Chas reappeared and interrupted her thoughts. She turned to look at him and realised just how tired he looked.

"Have you found him?" she whispered, moving towards him and away from her brother. He shook his head.

"The lorry neither. Everyone we've asked has seen neither sight nor sound of them."

"Will you charge him?" she asked.

He nodded.

"The Police think I should too. They say I'd be an idiot to let him go."

Guiding him into the corridor, out of hearing from Giles she, she spoke to him again.

"Do you have to? He'd be in so much trouble. I'd really think well of you if you didn't"

Whether the smile was meant to influence him or not wasn't clear. In fact, she was probably unaware she had done it she was so tired. But it caused him to smile and look down at her innocent face.

"We'll see," he said, clasping his hands in front of him, which was about all he could say on the matter at this stage. The last thing he intended was to increase the pressure mounting on Jenny with all her troubles, but much depended on how soon the Police found Jacob and the state his lorry was in. After all, he did need it for business, and had contracts to fulfill.

DARK    SECRETS


PART    TWO


ONE


  Jenny watched the small birds at play from her kitchen window, darting here

and there, amongst Hawthorn bush and Ash. Blue tits, chaffinch and robin, to

name but a few; and a black bird down there near the roots of the ash. She was a

solitary bird, with her brownish hue. Never raiding the round bread and fat balls

that Jenny hung amongst the tangled branches. She preferred to peck at

snippets, falling to the ground, discarded by the smaller birds. In her own time.

The other family members scoffed at Jenny, saying the birds could find their

own food. But she continued all the same. Her argument being that after a hard

winter, with fat and bread in their bellies, they could face the new year in far

better condition. And so rear strong, healthy young. She also gained great

pleasure from watching them. And now they had grown accustomed to her, she

could go out and replace the hand rolled balls of bread and fat amongst the

branches, and they would only fly a few feet away; always watching, but never

coming any closer. But still, what an achievement, she thought. They were still

wild creatures, but as time passed they knew she meant them no harm. She would whistle and talk to them, and they would seem to answer. And as she washed and dried the plates lying in her sink, she watched the birds and, as so often happened, her thoughts drifted away over the past six months.

The doctors in the Victoria Hospital at Fairford were amazed. They likened the constitution of her father to that of an ox. Two days after the accident he was sitting up in his bed, joking with the nurses, saying he had not really been asleep, but merely squinting at them through half closed eyes whenever they took the occasion to bend over him to adjust his blankets. Even the starchy matron, with her bright red hair and heaving bosoms, warmed to him, and there was a tear in her eye when he left. Jenny could not feel such warmth though. She recalled the night of the accident, when they were in the rear of the cattle lorry, when he looked up and said those five special words. Those words that meant so much to her. "I'm sorry, lass. Forgive me". And she was prepared to forgive him. Forgive him for everything. For every cut, every bruise, every memory. All of it. And not just because she was afraid he was dying. But because she was that type of girl. A kind girl, a trusting girl, a girl who was one in a million. And yet, for all that he said that night, not once since he woke from the accident had he ever once mentioned those five small important words again. Or expressed any kind of compassion for the pain and the suffering he had caused her. And when the doctors told him there was no serious injury to his spine, although he would have to take it easy for a while as it was badly bruised, he brushed away their comments in his usual brash manner, and with the assistance of a wheel chair guided by Chas, made his way to the little Austin 7 loaned by Zack and was driven home.

Jenny thought of Chas often, during those few days to and from the hospital. She felt they had grown close. He was so kind and considerate. Always put her and her feelings first. Never appeared to be in a rush to leave her. And that smile. A smile that would light up the heart of any woman. A smile that not only came from his lips but from his eyes. From where they say you can see a person's soul. And on one or two occasions she believed she may have seen right through to his soul. And what a man he was. Such a kind, friendly, happy man. One she could have spent the rest of her life with.

But then, as she held a plate between her hands, wiping it with the towel, she let out a long deep sigh and stared long and hard out of the window. Alas, it was not to be. Since that time, after the accident, she had seen little of Chas. Five, six times maybe. No more. And on each occasion, such a fleeting visit. More, she thought, to ask after the health of her father, than to ever mention his feelings towards her.

Or maybe the cause of it was Jacob, with his sarcastic smile. Always somewhere in the background to offer advise, whether it was needed or not. Chas and Jacob had never got on, not since the accident. She knew that. Chas had gone against the Police advice, and decided in his wisdom not to prosecute

Jacob. Whether it was the right thing to do or not, who could tell. True, she had pleaded with Chas at the hospital not to charge him. And he said he would have to see. Maybe that was the reason. And if it had been, did she wish she had not made the gesture. Maybe, maybe not. But who could say. The outcome was far from satisfactory. To the best of her knowledge Jacob had never thanked Chas for being lenient. In fact, he appeared to sneer at the other man whenever he called at the farm. As if itching for a fight. But Chas was known locally as being one who could hold his temper, and many a remark that was aimed in his direction, he decided to ignore.

And Giles. What of poor Giles. Little had changed for him. Other than more and more work being piled upon his young shoulders. He had shown great love and respect for his father at the hospital. Grief, even, that Jenny had never seen him display before. Other than when their mother left, all of four and a half years ago. And how had that grief been repaid. With her father shouting more and more at his younger son, taking the occasional swipe at him whenever he came too close. And Jacob barking never ending orders at the poor lad, now he was assuming more of the role as the bread winner. For try as Garnett might, he could not get around as he used to. Maybe he should have spent more time in the hospital; maybe he had been trying too hard. Whatever the reason, his back gave him great pain and he still hobbled around the house and the yard like an old man. Rarely making trips to market or to visit his dealer friends, which in turn made him cantankerous and considerably hard to live with.

So Jenny's life was not an easy one. And day after day seemed to knock her back once more into the submission she had known before the accident. Before she got to know Chas really well. And she felt a little bitter.

## TWO

The back door opened and she was brought back to reality. Jacob walked in and threw his jacket on the hook behind the door. It was late afternoon and the sun cast long grey shadows across the stone tiled floor.

"You watching them birds again?" he asked, sidling up alongside her near the sink, in a manner he seemed to use more frequently of late. The heat radiating from his body and the stench of sweat made her feel uncomfortable. For he had been working hard out in the fields. But, as she moved to one side away from him, so he would lean in that direction and cover her escape. He placed his large calloused hands on either side of the Belfast sink, and his strong arms brushed up against her sides. She was like a prisoner; unable to escape. His breathing was slow at first and she felt his hot breath up against her neck as he moved closer. And for a while they stood there, almost locked in an embrace. One of his making, not hers. His breathing was growing faster now, and she could feel his body drawing close to hers. His chest moving back and forth against her, in time with his breathing. Nodding towards one of the small free birds, safe amongst the hawthorn branches, he commented on how round and plump they had grown. And then he looked down at her chest. She was frightened. She felt this was wrong, but not sure why. She was being pushed closer and harder against the sink and there was no where else to turn.  He was breathing heavier now and she could feel his manhood growing larger and firmer against the small of her back. And this she could not understand. Why was this happening? She had seen her brother Giles naked when he was younger, when she helped bathed him with their mother. And she knew men and women, boys and girls, were different. Her mother had explained all that to her. And that she could understand. But why was Jacob growing hard like this. And what would it look like. She could only imagine. But those thoughts she quickly cast aside. She felt guilty for even thinking of them. She did not want him near her, towering above her. She wanted to be free. Like the small birds outside. Flying here and there, wherever they wished. But she was afraid. So very afraid. She had never experienced anything like this before. But she dare not shout. That would only annoy him. And then what. She had faced his anger on a number of occasions and she did not like it.

And then she saw him. The man who could save her. Coming across the yard. Towards the house. Thank God. At last. She knew she would be safe. For a while, at least.

"Dad's coming, from across the yard," she said in no more than a whisper. And for the first time in many a day she was pleased to see him. Jacob almost leapt away from the sink. Rushing across the room, he grabbed one of the chairs and placed it close against the table. Lowering his body onto it he said "Make him a pot of tea."

Jenny breathed in deeply, felt her knees go weak, and grabbed for the side of the sink.

"Now," snapped Jacob, adjusting the front of his trousers and leaning forward against the table so that the part of his body where his manhood lay could not be seen.

Gathering all her strength, the poor defenceless girl, still feeling faint, shuffled towards the range and began to prepare a pot of tea. Garnett opened the back door and shuffled in with the aid of his walking stick, an old knotted length of hawthorn that had grown dark and smooth over the years and cut to the appropriate size. He was like an old man now. He'd aged considerably over the past three months and looked far older than his fifty three years. His back was bent and his shoulders arched. So different now to how he used to stand, straight and tall.

Placing one hand to steady himself against the table he pulled out a chair and, with a grunt, lowered himself into it. Jacob watched, but said nothing. He was an independent man, was Garnett Couling, and woe betide the person who offered him assistance.

The two men discussed various aspects of the farm. What land needed the plough, where the best of the spring corn would grow, which field of grass was tall enough and dry enough to take the cattle. The sort of talk that would be of no interest at all to a man not connected with farming. But of vital importance to this father and son. Yet even, in the three short months since Garnett's accident, the attitude was changing between the pair. Whereas before, Jacob would bow to his fathers greater experience, and take heed of what needed to be done, now he would question almost every decision that Garnett made. Whether it was sheer cussedness, or he was, at last, taking an interest in the farm, was hard to say. But he was going out to the pubs less and less, and spending far more time working in the fields and around the yard. And that was not to everyone's advantage.

"What's up with you, girl?" growled Garnett, turning towards Jenny as she placed two mugs of steaming hot tea on the table. Jacob stared long and hard at her, but said nothing. For a fleeting moment she glanced back at him, but could not hold the stare. Instead, she lowered her gaze to the ground.

"You look as pale as a sheet. You not well or something?"

She shook her head and glanced at him before looking back down at the ground. She knew she must choose her words carefully with Jacob still in the room.

"I've had a belly ache most of the day," she lied. "Must have eaten something that didn't suite me."

She wished she had the nerve to tell the truth. But she knew there was little chance of that, and so did Jacob.

"Well, you'd best get the milking done, feed your stock, make our tea and then get yourself off to bed. Don't want you knocking yourself up, do we?"

"No Dad," she replied, without raising her eyes from the ground. Shuffling over to the door she grabbed the shawl her granny used to wear and made her way to the cowshed. Dog met her outside and followed. He too had changed. No longer did he spend all his time with Garnett. Whenever his owner was not around he would follow Jenny, and often sidle up against her for a stroke, or lick her leg affectionately. Maybe he realised from the night of the accident, when she covered him with a blanket by the fire, that she had compassion. Something Garnett never showed.

"Good boy," she whispered, bending over and patting his head after she had opened the cowshed door.

"Let's go and get the cattle."

Dog had learnt in a very short space of time that this part of the day spelt fun. Something he had not been used to with Garnett. The five milking cows and two in calf heifers were a field away beyond the one at the back of the cowshed. That one had been poached during the winter season, was still damp and needed time to recover. The dog and the girl walked into the first meadow and Dog galloped away in the general direction of the cows. Jenny picked up a broken twig, and as with every day, her companion sensed this, turned and galloped towards her. He was a big ugly beast, a mongrel of some description, but in the main he seemed to favour on the side of the lurcher. But for all his ugliness, with a wall eye to the right and half an ear to the left of his face, Jenny had grown fond of the brute, and he of her. And somewhere in that big ugly face was a look that made her feel warm inside. Leaping, jumping and frothing in front of her he would have laughed had he been human, and she laughed too. She threw the twig and watched as he loped after it, and as she watched, she smiled. Why oh why, she thought, could humans not be like animals. Kind, considerate. Only needing love, and always prepared to hand it back ten fold in return.

As he returned she made him sit, which he did reluctantly. She made him drop the twig, again which he did not want to do. And as he sat there looking up at her as she teased him with the twig she said with a smile "I think I may draw you one day. If you don't mind."

If the old dog understood her words he showed little sign of it. Instead, grabbing the twig from her hand, he darted off again and she chased after him, chastising him as she ran, laughing aloud and not caring if any one heard them as they played.

# THREE

The rest of the week passed swiftly, and, although Jacob gave her some odd

looks, Jenny managed to keep out of his way most of the time. Garnett hollered

and bellowed at all of his children at different times and once, when Giles was

taking too long tying his father's boot laces, a task that had befallen to him of

late since his father could not bend too well, he received a clout around the side

of the head, delivered by the hawthorn stick. The blow was savage and hard,

and a lesser child would have screamed aloud; but Giles was built of stronger

stuff and merely grimaced. However, Jenny still noticed a trickle of blood

escape from his ear and run down his cheek. She offered to wipe it for him with

a cloth, but he pushed her away and ran outdoors, where he could deal with his

pain alone.

Saturday arrived, much like any other Saturday and Jenny carried out her

chores with the usual dedication she applied to most things. Giles had suffered

severe headaches since the cuff around the side of his head, and reluctantly

Garnett had agreed he could spend a few hours in bed, much against the wishes

of Jacob, who cursed and swore and told everyone it meant he would have to

carry out Giles share of the work by himself. But it cut no ice with Garnett, and

still being the head of the household, his word was final.

As morning drifted into afternoon, Jenny longed for time alone. Where she could think her innermost thoughts. When no one was around, and all was quiet, she left the confines of the farmyard and, with Dog at her heels, walked slowly across three acre meadow. He sensed she was quiet for a reason and walked quietly by her side, occasionally snapping at a fly or insect that flew too near. There was a gentle rise from the farmyard to the boundary fence, at the top of which stood a small copse in which she could loose herself. If the rest of the family knew she came here, they never mentioned it.

As she settled down, to be alone with Dog and think, she stared out beyond the Lechlade road, towards the River Thames, meandering slowly amongst open fields of lush green pasture. Cows grazed in some; sheep in others, and she smiled. With the sun warming her pale, soft features, she leant back and rested on outstretched arms, lifting her face skywards. Closing her eyes she thought of happier times. When she was a young child, when her mother still lived at Holly Bank Farm. And many thoughts drifted in and out of her mind.

She was almost asleep, at that stage when the brain is neither conscious nor unconscious, when she felt something warm and hard resting against her thigh. At first it felt pleasant. Nice and warm. Nothing untoward. Something she would not mind resting against her as she fell into a deep and tranquil sleep. Of no consequence. Yet as her brain drifted slowly towards the conscious rather than the subconscious, she tried hard to imagine what it could be. And the harder she tried, the more difficult it became. Not only to try and discover what it was, but to pull herself back into the real world. Her body was relaxed now, her eyes warm and comfortable from the heat of the sun. She didn't want to return to the real world. She only wanted to drift away. Into a world of her own. Where she was safe. But if she was to discover what this object was, then she must make the effort. She must force herself. And as she pushed herself back into the early stages of consciousness, so the object moved. Barely noticeable, but enough for her to know that by the slight decrease of pressure and then more pressure, that it had moved farther up her thigh. She did not understand. Why should it do that? For what possible reason. All this thinking and guessing took little more than a few seconds, but to a mind that was that near to sleep, it could have lasted hours. Forcing sleep farther from her mind, thoughts of the present came back to her. Places, people, faces, names. And one face kept drifting nearer and nearer, only to drift away again, like on the mists of time. Only this time, the final time, it remained. As clear as if it had been real. The face of her brother. The one man who scared her more than even her father. His name was Jacob.

Screaming aloud, she leapt forward into the air and, with eyes darting this way and that, searched all around the copse for him. He had to be there. Somewhere. If not visible, then hiding somewhere in amongst the newly grown brush or the evergreen branches. With her breasts heaving, her body twisting this way and that, she searched desperately. Down amongst the undergrowth, up amongst the trees. But all to no avail. He must have run off, like a coward in the night. To hide and strike again.

Yet slowly, as the seconds passed into minutes, she gradually calmed herself and looked around. There was no sign of anyone. No sight, no sound. Only Dog. Looking up at her like an old friend. Confused. Unsure. For a while she stared down at him and he up at her. And gradually, very gradually, the truth dawned on her. It was him. It had to be him. And letting out a mighty sigh of relief, she laughed aloud, knelt down and threw her arms about the dog's neck. And he in turn licked her face. What a fool she had been. Would any man, let alone Jacob, ever attempt to harm her when her beloved Dog was nearby. She thought not. And as she lowered herself slowly once more onto the ground, the faithful old animal lay down peacefully beside her and laid his head once more upon her thigh.

# FOUR

Later that afternoon, after Jenny had milked the cows, fed the chicken and completed the hundred and one other chores she was expected to carry out around the farm, she was in the parlour preparing tea. Jacob was whittling a lump of wood from an ash tree; Giles was reading a book on Spain and Garnett was snoring in his favourite leather backed arm chair. Dog, who was not classed as a family pet by anyone apart from Jenny, was tied up outside to a wooden barrel that served as a kennel. As normal, he was the first to hear the arrival of any visitors, and began to bark as Harry Dawson pulled up into the yard in his latest acquisition, a bright red Morris Cowley " Bullnose " convertible. The colour matched his personality, for he was a loud and jovial man, and the weather, being so fine that day, meant that he could drive along with the hood down, with not a care in the world.

Garnett awoke from his slumber.

"What's that damn dog barking at now?" He cursed.

Jenny, looking through the parlour window, recognised Harry's car.

"It's Mister Dawson," she said with the same respect she gave to any grown up.

"And he's got Alice with him," she said excitedly, rubbing her hands clean on her apron and hanging it on the hook behind the back door.

Jacob looked up from his whittling. He knew Alice, although he had not seen her for a number of months, and like Jenny, he knew she was growing into a fine looking lass. The two girls had been firm friends since they were youngsters and Jenny was always pleased to see Alice, for it used to mean that she would stay over for the night. Whether she would now, though, was still to be seen. Harry Dawson was a prosperous beef farmer and cattle dealer around these parts and up until recently had owned a fair sized farm on the Lechlade to Fairford road. Round about the time of Garnett's accident, though, he sold that one and bought a larger farm out Cirencester way. In fact, Jenny remembered that Chas had got the job of moving the herd a week or so after the accident. She recalled it took him a number of days.

Jenny opened the back door for their guests and told Dog to be quiet, although he took no notice. Harry walked in first, smiled at Jenny and crossed the parlour to meet her father. He was a large man, not unlike Garnett, but so different in every other way. Cheery, always smiling, and never a bad word for any one. Well, maybe one or two. But not that many. And he always seemed to be so kind to his daughter. Oh how Jenny wished she could have a father like that. But she realised it was not to be.

The two girls gave each other a hug and Alice handed her friend a small posy of primroses. Jenny was delighted. It may have been a small gift, especially to town folk, but out here in the country it was the thought that counted and that meant so much.

The two girls crossed to the sink and Jenny placed them in water. Jacob watched them silently, and though they were not aware of this, Giles was, and wondered why.

"So, how've you been keeping, then?" asked Harry of his old friend, as he pulled up a vacant chair and lowered his large frame down into it. The two of them had been constant companions in their youth, and that friendship had lasted over all these years. If Harry had known how cruel Garnett could be to his children, then it might have been a different story. But like all bullies, Garnett managed to hide his misdemeanours well, and at worst Harry thought he may be a little harsh on his children. But no more. And there were many a man he knew who was far worse than that.

Garnett explained that he was still not feeling right, and still suffered a great deal since the accident. His lower back gave him jip most days, and there was not too much feeling in his right leg, which caused him to limp.

Harry suggested that he ought to make a return visit to the hospital, but Garnett would have none of it, and continued to moan about his ill health and other worries until Jenny arrived with pork sandwiches and mugs of tea.

Harry thanked her kindly with a smile and said how much she had grown and what a fine looking girl she was turning into. She blushed, thanked him and scurried away with Alice up to her bedroom, there to have girly talk with her friend.

As the men devoured their sandwiches, Harry was surprised in the change that had taken place in his friend and told him so. Garnett, on the other hand, would have none of it.

"You may disagree," said Harry. "But I'm telling you here and now. You're a miserable old bugger, and no mistake. Christ, you haven't sopped moaning since I got here, and that has to be a good twenty minutes or so."

"And don't I have enough to moan about," replied Garnett. "This place doesn't run itself, you know."

"It doesn't have to," replied Harry, picking up another sandwich. Pointing to Jacob he said "You've got a fine looking lad there who can run most of it for you."

"And a lot of bloody good he is," moaned Garnett, staring at his elder son.

"If I tell him to do one thing, then he wants to do the opposite. We spend half the bloody day arguing before he ever gets anything done."

Jacob looked daggers at his father. He stopped whittling, placed the ash wood on the table and stared back across the table, stroking the knife between his hands. This attitude between father and son surprised Harry. Until recently they always seemed to get on well together. Not so now. Harry smiled with that broad grin of his that seemed to light up the whole of his face.

"Not to worry," he said, tapping the other man on the arm.

"I've got the perfect cure. In fact, that's why I came over here this evening."

"Oh ah," mumbled Garnett, taking a last gulp of tea from his mug. "And what might that be?"

"Well, I've not been over this way much since I moved to Cirencester. Thought I'd have a small reunion with a few of me friends. So I've booked in overnight at The Bull in Fairford and apart from you, I've arranged for half a dozen of them to meet me in there tonight for a few pints."

Garnett didn't seem too pleased, and Harry noticed this. There was a time, before the accident, that Garnett would have jumped at the chance for a bit of a do. Especially if there were likely to be a few free beers. But now he had taken to drinking more at home. And retired early to his bed. And he told Harry so.

Harry grinned.

"So that's just the reason why you could do with a night out," he said. "It'll do you good, and besides, the rest of the lads would be pleased to see you."

Garnett still declined the offer, but, being a successful dealer , Harry was used to persuading people to carry out his wishes, and his friend was no exception. When Harry said that his room at the Bull was a double and Garnett could spend the night there if he had too much ale to drink, and he would bring him back in the morning, then what else was there to say. Harry slapped him on the shoulder, which caused him to wince, and said he was doing the right thing.

"I was thinking of leaving our Alice here overnight," he said, refilling his mug with tea from the pot. "If that's all right with you."

Whilst Garnett said that he could see no objection, Jacob looked past them towards the stairs and had a strange look in his eyes. And again, Giles noticed this, but said nothing

The girls were called down later and given the good news as the two men prepared to leave. Alice gave her father a big hug and a kiss as he held her close to him. By contrast, Jenny stood with hands clasped in front of her white cotton skirt and merely said "night Dad," as he left the room. If he did reply, then she never heard it, and he did not repeat himself..

# FIVE

Once their fathers had gone, the two girls ran back up stairs again to Jenny's bedroom; and from the comfort of his chair Jacob watched them go. Closing the door behind them, they leapt onto the bed and chuckled and giggled about all manner of innocent things that girls do of that age. Having a friend stay overnight was a great thrill for Jenny, and on these occasions, which were rare, she almost felt like a normal girl again. No knot in her stomach when she thought of her father, or the added fear of Jacob, who was acting very strange towards her of late.

Eventually the giggling died down and they began to talk of more serious things. How Alice was enjoying her new life over at Cirencester. On the big farm that was more than six hundred acres. It sounded like she was enjoying it very much. Her family of four, a mother, a father, a brother and an elderly aunt, all seemed quite normal. Also loving and caring. And the seven bedroom house and grounds were enormous. Very different from the Couling family, Jenny thought. All members of Alice's family adored her, for she was a very sweet child with a happy countenance. Confident, but not brash; ready to help, but never too pushy. The type of girl that Jenny naturally warmed to. And that was why they had remained friends over the years.

"Your hair looks like it could do with a brush," said Alice, in such a way that she did not offend. Taking the hair brush from a stool in the corner, she sat down behind Jenny, curled up on the bed, and began to brush her long golden locks in a slow, gentle manner that the older girl by a few months, cherished. For a while they remained silent. Jenny closed her eyes and relaxed, more than she had done for a very long time. Maybe since the last time Alice had stayed overnight. Alice was the first to speak.

"So, how are things with you now?"

Jenny remained silent. She knew exactly what Alice was referring to. But she preferred not to discuss it. Just to enjoy the sensation of the brush drifting through her hair, lightly brushing against her scalp was enough. If there was anything more enjoyable, then right now, as of this moment, she could not recall it. But Alice, although a kindly girl, was still a persistent one.

"Well?" She asked, in a voice that sounded firmer than before.

Jenny knew she must answer and drew in a deep breath.

"Much the same," she replied.

Alice stiffened slightly and this was transmitted through the handle of the brush, through the bristle and down onto Jenny's scalp. The sensation was ever so slight, but enough for Jenny to notice it.

"In other words it's got worse," she said.

Again Jenny said nothing. This was something she did not want to discuss. When she told Alice on her last visit that her father had abused her, she naively expected that would be the end of the matter. It would go away.  But it was not to be. When the awful truth came out, Alice said she had suspected as much for some years. Both from signs she had witnessed when Jenny changed into her night dress as they prepared for bed whenever she visited, and the way she had reacted in front of her father whenever he raised his voice. All pointed to a situation between father and daughter that all was not well.

In fairness to Alice, she had remained silent on the subject, so as not to cause her friend unnecessary stress. Leaving it for her to bring up the subject. But as time passed, and there was no sign that Jenny would talk of her secret, Alice decided that she would have to broach the subject herself. And how glad she was in one way, and so sad in another. For, after the flood of tears, that lasted well into the night, she felt Jenny was greatly relieved and could face the world with far more confidence, knowing she had confided in a friend. On the other hand, it disturbed her greatly to see her friend in so much pain, as she relived the horror and the terror of those past years. And knowing, only too well, that in those days, when the female of the species, had so little influence over their lives, there was nothing that Jenny could do. Other than agreeing to Alice informing her own father, who, being such a good and just man, would soon find a solution to the problem. But of course, Jenny would hear none of it; and swore her friend to secrecy. Alice had to agree. So now, having taken a child's oath of sorts, there was little Alice could do, other than plead with her friend to change her mind.

"Well?" asked Alice again, determined to press the subject.

"Is it worse than it was, or not?"

"No," lied Jenny. "It's much the same."

"I don't believe you," said Alice,

"Well, it's the truth," replied Jenny, rather feebly.

Alice laid down the brush on the bed and kneeling up, she pulled Jenny around to face her.

"Look at me, straight in the eye," she ordered, and reluctantly, Jenny felt compelled to obey.

"I'm right, aren't I?" she said, and Jenny looked down at the freshly laundered blanket she had laid across the bed earlier that day. And she remembered the dream she had of Jacob, up on the copse that afternoon.

"It's not much worse," said Jenny, tears welling up in her eyes. She decided she would only talk about her father; and hope Jacob would go away in time.

"But it's still going on," She added.

Alice stared at her friend. She had known in her heart it was true. But she hoped it was not. She grabbed Jenny with both arms and pulled her close. She must help her all she could.

"You poor thing," she whispered, as their heads pressed one against the other, the contrast of the black and gold strands of hair from the two girls mingling together. And Jenny felt so safe. Here she was with Alice, a good and trusted friend, and she began to sob. Slowly at first, with little gasps of air sucked in through her nose. And tears began to roll down her cheeks, into small rivulets that twisted this way and that around her chin. But the more she sobbed, the less she was able to control herself. Soon she was taking in great gulps of air through her mouth, unable to stop, and she pushed her face deeper and deeper into Alice's shoulder, desperate to soak up the love, support and security, that was now being offered by her friend.

Alice clung to her as the minutes ticked by, feeling so sad on the one hand, yet so bitter and angry on the other. How could any man be like this. So hard and cruel. True, she had heard stories of brutality around these parts. And often it was accepted as a way of life. For were not women treated as the chattels of men. But to see this, her close friend, in tears and so upset. This was different. This was first hand. And maybe the truth hurt even more and was harder to accept because her own father, Harry Dawson, was such a kind and considerate man. A man who cared for and loved all his family; his wife, his children and his older sister who lived with them. Even his dogs, his horses and his cattle. He would never have any person raise a stick to them. And the story went that on one occasion, when he walked around the corner of his yard he came across one of his carters. The man was just about to raise his whip in anger at a shire horse, stiff and troubled with age, whereupon Harry grabbed the man, threw him into a stone trough full of water and gave the man a good dousing. Once satisfied the fellow had calmed down, Harry, who was a big man, pulled him out of the trough with one hand and whipped him all the way down the driveway with the other. And when the man had the gall to return a few days later for his wages, Harry, who was an honest man, bundled a few notes into his pocket and whipped him off down the driveway again for good measure. And the man never did return again.

Yet Alice was sure her father never suspected Mr. Couling to be such a tyrant. Or he would never have been friends with the man. Of that she was sure. So, what was the alternative. She could not tell her father of Jenny's predicament, of that she was certain. Jenny had sworn her to secrecy in the past, and she was not likely to change her views now, however bad the beatings became. For Jenny was scared; really scared. And any mention of such a plan would only make her worse. And Alice could not cause her more hardship.

"I was thinking," she said, as her friends breathing slowly returned to normal. "Why don't you come over and stay with us for a few days. It would be like a holiday, and it would give you a few days away from him. Also you could see where we live now."

Jenny sniffed, took the handkerchief from Alice and wiped her eyes. Shaking her head slowly she said "No. I couldn't do that. He wouldn't let me."

Alice paused for a moment.

"He would if my Dad asked him," she said, seeing the merest hint of hope rising from this desperate situation. Jenny blew her nose and sniffed.

"He wouldn't. He'd only say he'd need me here to do the milking, look after the chickens and run the house. I know he would."

"You can't be sure of that," pleaded Alice, knowing she would have to knock all these excuses on the head as they arose.

"I am." Replied Jenny. "I know my Dad, you don't"

"But he can't expect you to be here all the time." Argued Alice.

Jenny perched back on her haunches on the bed, slightly more composed.

"He can," she replied. "And now he can't get about so well, he'll expect it even more."

They both paused for a while and Jenny looked down once more at the blanket covering the bed.

"But that's not fair," said Alice, folding her arms in front of her.

"Life's not fair," muttered Jenny, clasping her hands together. "And it never has been for me. Not since Mum left."

As thoughts of happier days flashed through her mind she burst into tears once more and Alice leant forward to console her.

# SIX

Jacob stirred in his chair and rubbed his eyes. He'd been dozing in the parlour for the past hour but it was a fitful sleep. One where images drifted to and fro across the mind. Rarely to leave. And if they do, it is only to return once more, far stronger than before. Images that pleased him; excited him. Of the two young girls upstairs in their bed. Dressed only in thin cotton shifts. In their prime, at sixteen. One his sister, the other, her friend. Both ready to be deflowered and he was the man to do it.

As he thought of his sister, he craved for her young, supple body. Probably more so than her friend. He knew it was wrong; and that made it all the more exciting. In the past he had tried to curb his yearnings; those base, carnal cravings when first he reached puberty. Until then he had taken little notice of her. She was plain, skinny with a pale skin. He had vied for more striking girls, the likes of Tammy over at the Nags Head. But hadn't she spurned him. On every occasion he made advances, she would ridicule him. Just like all the other girls. Why, only six months ago, when he was over there tiling her father's roof, hadn't she made him look a fool in front of a complete stranger when she ridiculed his manhood and said he couldn't even satisfy a pigmy. God, how he hated her; how he hated all women. Even his Mother, whom he had not seen for the past four years, since he was seventeen.

He would never forget that day. It was a winter's day. Cold and frosty, with a good layer of snow across the ground. And the sky was grey, that sort of miserable day that shows the end of winter is still a long way off. He'd been out in the fields alone, cutting back and repairing a hawthorn hedge that had grown bare in places, allowing the stock to break through. He enjoyed hedging. It was a lonesome occupation, but one with which he could cope. Where, if in a bad mood, which he often was, he could lay into thick solid branches and knock hell out of them with a billhook 'till they split. He enjoyed that. With no sun to help him in the sky, he guessed it was somewhere around mid day, and he was ready for a mug of tea to warm him up, along with a good bowl of stew to fill his stomach.

Taking the billhook with him, for he had spent some time carving the handle to suit his own particular grasp, he crossed the meadow and came up on the yard. His brother and sister would still be at school over at Buscot, and his father should still be at market, for there was no sign of the truck he always parked up near the back door to the house. There was, however, a small black Austin 7 parked outside the gateway of the farm, on the Lechlade to Buscot road, but he paid it no heed, expecting the owner to be in the house visiting. .

Opening the back door, he entered the parlour and was about to remove his coat and cap, when he was confronted by a sight that life had not prepared him for. At seventeen, he was a large lad, but somewhat immature, and for a while

118

he stood there, gazing, with an open mouth. Was he really seeing this, or was it something in his imagination. His mother, his very own mother, the wife of his father, standing there, close to the range, wrapped in the arms of another man. He shook his head. Could this really be happening? A red mist rose in his eyes. The man, balding and in his forties, was staring back at him; his mother was facing the man. She must have felt some reaction from her lover, for as Jacob tightened his grip on the billhook, so she turned around to face him.

The billhook was high in the air now, razor sharp on the leading edge. And while mother and son stood staring at each other, all time seemed to stand still. His initial thoughts were of hate, revenge, even death. To one or both of them. He did not care which. They had deceived him. She had rejected his love and his family's love for another man. And the man had taken her love from that family. Yet what he could not understand was the look in his mother's eyes, her face, her whole being. True, she was dressed in a black winter's coat with her favourite blue scarf tied about her head, and a leather suitcase laying near her feet. But she was almost serene. Although she faced his wrath and the fate of the billhook, he knew it did not matter to her. For once in her miserable life she was happy. Really happy. She was with a man whom she loved, and that man loved her. And in that instant, in that millisecond, when untold carnage could occur if Jacob were to wield the billhook, it did not matter to her. She had found her love.

After years of beatings and abuse from his father she had finally found a release. And either that release could be a life together with her lover, or death with him here, in this grubby little farmhouse, which she had tried to make a home; but had failed. And did it really matter what happened. Whichever way it went, it would be over soon. Either she would have a new life, or a new after life. It mattered not. The choice was his. Her son. He must make the decision and make it now.

# SEVEN

Jenny was the first to arrive in the parlour, shortly followed by Alice. Together the two girls prepared breakfast, and once it was laid out on the table, Jenny shouted from the foot of the stairs for her brothers to come down. Giles was the first to arrive, with tousled hair and the odd yawn, and took his place at the table.

"This looks good," he said, deciding which part of his plate to attack first as he studied the bacon, ham and eggs set out before him, all balanced precariously on a perfectly browned slice of fried bread.

"Most of that's Alice's work," smiled Jenny, sipping tea from her mug.

Giles smiled as best he could at Alice, without loosing too much of the large lump of bacon that he had crammed into his mouth. It was hot and greasy, and very tasty; and he was not going to waste a bit of it. Alice carried her mug across from the range and joined them.

"Is Jacob awake yet?" she asked, cutting a small piece of fried bread and dipping it into the egg yoke on her plate, before placing it delicately into her mouth.

Giles swallowed his bacon and said "He was snoring like a good 'un when I came down. I doubt if he'll be up for a while yet."

"He'd better had be," smiled Alice, deciding which tasty morsel she would eat next. "We put a lot of effort into this, didn't we, Jenny?"

Jenny nodded, although in truth, it was no more and no better than she usually served up for them on a Sunday. But if Giles thought Alice's cooking was better than hers, then so be it.

All three children ate in silence for a while, each enjoying what was on their plate. Giles enjoyed everything that had been offered, whereas Alice liked the egg best. Jenny, who was not a big eater, picked at hers, and cast her mind back to last night. How she had cried in pain in front of her friend, and how her friend had cuddled her. Of the fear whenever she thought of her father who beat her; or of Jacob who fondled her. But there were also memories of happier times, whenever she thought of her Mother, who would brush her hair, just like Alice had done last night. But in a way these memories were tinged with sadness as she recalled the time of her Mother's leaving. The suddenness of it all. How she had been at school all day, and when she returned home with Giles, a mere eight year old, in the afternoon, and entered the house, there was only one person there. Not their Mother, whom they would have expected. But their seventeen year old brother, Jacob. Sitting alone in the parlour, dried tear stains down his cheeks and a vacant look about his face. And in that instant, as she entered the house, she knew in her heart that her mother was not there. The house felt empty; as though it had lost its very soul. The one person who could make that house a home had left and she knew it. When she asked of Jacob what had happened, he just sat there in silence. And when she pushed him further, with her face up to his, he slapped her hard, so she fell back against the table and he walked from the room, leaving the pair of them to guess their mothers fate

Not until later that night, much later, did they hear the truth. From their father, who had finally gleaned the truth from Jacob. And when he told them, it was a simple affair. He called them to the parlour from their rooms upstairs, had them stand in front of him and simply said "You'd best know, your Mothers left. The cow has left me for another man." Giles did not fully understand the gravity of what had been said. How could he, he was only eight. But when Jenny tried to push Garnett further, as she had with Jacob, he treated her in much the same way. Except that he did not leave the room. He beat her once, he beat her twice, and then he beat her some more. And when Giles cried, he beat him too. And then he yelled for both of them to get out of his sight and back up to their rooms.

That was how Jenny learnt of her Mother's leaving. As basic as that. No frills, no finery. No thought of easing her pain. Just a few simple words, delivered in a gruff voice she had become accustomed to over the years. But that was how her father was. And it was only as time passed that she could understand why her Mother had left. For she now received the beatings that her Mother had received. And she too could understand, at last, why her Mother would have left with a man she loved. Would not she do the very same, if she could find such a man.

Her thoughts were interrupted when Alice rose for her chair and walked towards the stairs.

"Where are you going?" She asked.

Alice turned to face her.

"Honest, Jenny. Don't you ever listen. I just told you, I was going up to wake that brother of yours. If he doesn't come down soon, his breakfast will be cold."

A vision of Alice standing in Jacob's room brought sudden panic to the young girl.

"No!" She almost screamed, with such force that Giles jerked his head in her direction. Even Alice turned as Jenny leapt from the table, and wondered what had possessed her friend. Jenny had always been a pale girl, but now she looked as though she had seen a ghost. Suddenly aware that she had reacted with much more force than intended, she tried to compose herself, and gave a false smile.

"It's all right," she said, quietly now. "I'll go," and began to cross the room.

"Don't be silly," replied Alice, turning back towards the stairs.

"I've nearly finished my breakfast. You've got nearly a whole plateful to get through yet."

Jenny looked down at the table, aware that Giles was still watching her, and realised she had hardly touched her food. There was little she could do without giving her secret away. She must let Alice go, and pray to God that Jacob would not defile her in any way. At least he knew there were others in the house, and that may save her.

Returning to her seat, Jenny listened as Alice's footsteps creaked on loose steps leading up the stair case. Giles shrugged and, ripping a sizable chunk of bread from the loaf, began mopping up egg yoke and bacon fat from his plate. Jenny watched him for a moment and then her eyes drifted towards the stairs.

After what seemed an eternity, as Alice's footsteps drifted nearer and nearer to Jacob's room, she suddenly heard her call out before she reached the door.

"Jacob, if you don't get up now, we'll throw your breakfast out to the pigs. And I mean it."

If a crowd had been in the parlour, then the look of sheer and utter relief on Jenny's face would have been plain for all to see. As it was, however, Giles was the only one present, and he was preoccupied with cleaning his plate. He only looked up as Alice returned to the room and took up her seat again at the table.

## EIGHT

Later that morning, with breakfast out of the way, the cows milked and the chickens fed, Alice and Jenny were enjoying themselves taking a walk across the fields. Dog was running along by there side, waiting for one of them to throw a stick for him. As they were deep in conversation, and taking little notice, he began to bark. Alice, who was still holding the  stick, threw it away, and watched him gallop off after it, like some great cart horse, swaying from side to side.

"He is a big clumsy dog," she laughed, grabbing her bonnet as a gust of wind tried in vain to pull it from her grasp.

"And so ugly," she added, as he turned around and revealed the wall eye on the right side of his face and the half ear to the left.

Jenny was slightly hurt, but didn't say anything. She had grown to love Dog, even if she had to agree that he was ugly.

"He's very faithful," she protested. "Especially to me."

"I'm sure he is," smiled Alice, taking the stick from him and throwing it again.

"But he's not the sort of dog you could take out visiting with you anywhere, is he."

"And why not?" Asked Jenny, with a measured amount of indignation in her voice.

"Well, everyone would laugh at him, wouldn't they?"

"They would not," snapped Jenny. "And if they did, I'd tell them just what I thought of them."

Alice turned to her friend and shook her head.

"If only that were true, Jenny. But you know, and I know that would never happen."

For a moment she paused, then added "You're too nice a person to do that."

Jenny wasn't too sure whether that was meant to be a back handed compliment, or just another way of Alice getting out of a spot. The trouble was though; she knew it to be true. And only in her dreams would she ever stand up and face anyone.

Coming to a sudden halt she turned to Alice and said " I really do wish I was like you. You don't seem to be scared of anyone. And you say exactly what you think."

Alice threw the stick a third time for Dog and turned to her friend.

"You only have to have confidence. Start to believe in yourself."

"How do you mean?" Asked Jenny.

Alice thought for a moment.

"Well, think of something that you're really good at... Let every one see that you're good at it, and then you'll believe in it yourself."

Jenny looked down at some wild daisies growing in amongst the grass.

"I'm not good at anything," she said with sorrow in her voice.

"There must be something," said Alice. "Everyone has got at least one thing they're good at."

"Well, I haven't," replied Jenny.

Alice paused a moment ant thought. Then she said "There must be something you really like doing. That gives you a great deal of pleasure."

Just then Dog bounded over and knocked into Jenny with such force that she fell to the ground, and as she lay there she laughed aloud as Dog began to lick her.

"I enjoy taking him for walks and having him around me," she laughed aloud as his tongue tickled her face. "And I know I'll enjoy drawing him when I get round to it" she added as an afterthought.

Alice looked most surprised and knelt down on the ground beside her.

"Draw. Draw him. What are you talking about?" She asked.

It was only then that Jenny realised she had let slip her secret.

"Oh, nothing," she replied.

"What do you mean, Nothing?" Asked Alice, peering down into her bright blue eyes. "You said you could draw him. So you must be able to draw."

Jenny thought for a minute.

"Well, I can draw. A little bit. But not that well."

Alice rose to her feet and dragged Jenny up with her.

"Come on my girl," she said. "You're coming with me."

"Where are we going?" asked Jenny, wiping the grass from her clean white skirt.

"We're going back to the house and your going to show me these drawings of yours. That's what we're going to do."

"Oh no," protested Jenny. "We can't do that, they're not that good."

"It doesn't matter," said Alice. "I want to have a look at them anyway."

And with that, she dragged her friend, still protesting, back to the house, with Dog lolloping along at their heels.

Fortunately the parlour was empty when they arrived. Either Jacob and Giles were outside or up in their rooms. Not that it mattered much to Alice. She was not the least bit scared of Jacob. Besides, she was desperately excited to see Jenny's work. Together they climbed the stairs, although Jenny was under some apprehension as she entered her room and closed the door behind Alice.

"Well," asked her friend eagerly. "Where are they?"

Already Jenny was having second thoughts.

"Are you sure you want to see them. Really sure?"

"Of course I am," replied Alice, sitting on the bed and watching Jenny kneel down by her side and reach under the overhanging blanket.

Jenny looked up at her friend and said "You will promise you'll never tell anyone I keep them here," she pleaded, and of course, Alice agreed.

Reaching for the handle, she pulled out a small leather case with the initials "AM" embossed on the front in black, and placed it on the bed.

"Whose initials are those?" Asked Alice.

Jenny looked at them for a moment and remembered the initials with pride.

"My mother's," she replied. "Her name, before she was married."

"What do they stand for," asked Alice.

"Amanda Beckworth," replied Jenny, with a genuine smile.

"That's a nice name," said Alice, eager now to look in the case.

Jenny nodded. "It is, isn't it?"

Slowly Jenny released the metal clasp and raised the lid. The whole case measured no more than two foot long and one foot wide and was about six inches deep. Lifting a linen cloth from inside, she revealed the contents, and Alice gasped and covered her mouth with her hands in surprise. There, staring back at her, was the drawing of a goldfinch, the likes of which she had never seen before. It was not a very large drawing, of a bird with both its feet resting between the thorns on the branch of a hawthorn tree, and the colour of its head was shaded black and white, with a hint of red chalk rubbed in above its crown. Yellow flashes along its side wings and a touch of brown along its back.

"What?" Asked Jenny, not quite sure what to make of Alice's reaction.

Neither girl spoke for a moment. Alice, because she was so astonished she was unable to. Jenny, because she wanted Alice to like the drawing, but not at all sure whether she did.

"You don't like it, do you?" she said, slightly hurt. She didn't think her drawings were that good, but in her heart of hearts she did think they deserved some merit.

"Not like it!" gasped Alice, finally, finding her voice. "Not like it. It's the most wonderful drawing I've ever seen."

At last there was some positive reaction from Jenny. The corners of her eyes turned upwards and the centres began to sparkle. She climbed up onto the bed alongside her friend.

"Can I take it out and have a closer look?" asked Alice, desperate to hold it in her hands.

Jenny nodded; surprised that Alice should even need to ask. Taking hold of one corner, Alice gently lifted the drawing from the case and held it carefully between her hands.

"I just can't believe you drew this," she said at length.

"When did you first start drawing?"

"Soon after Mum left," replied Jenny, delving back into the case to retrieve some more sketches.

"She used to draw herself, and must have forgotten this case when she left. I found it hidden away in one of the cupboards down stairs when I was doing some cleaning. There wasn't much in it. Just a few pencils and one or two of her drawings. That's what I started copying from."

As one drawing was brought out, followed by another, Alice was just overwhelmed. She had some idea of good paintings because her father owned a small collection he had gathered over the years, and would occasionally take Alice to one or two of the posh galleries in London. And Alice really loved some of the paintings she saw there.

"Would you like to see the ones Mum left behind?" Jenny asked, unrolling a length of linen from the bottom of the case. Alice could not wait to see. As the first sketch came to view, Alice was bowled over. Staring back at her was a mirror image of Jenny, when she was no more than ten or eleven years old. Shaded so delicately in pencil, the hair falling about her shoulders, the magic in the eyes. So full of life and so different to how they were now. Everything had been captured in that portrait, of a child drawn by a mother, who loved her very much. A true bond, that could never be broken.

And still there were more. Jenny casually pulled out three more sketches, and instantly Alice recognised two. One was of Jacob, the second of Giles. And although they were exquisitely drawn, they could not match the love and the tenderness of the sketch that portrayed Jenny.

"I don't know who this is," said Jenny, handing the fourth and final sketch over to her friend. "It must have been a friend of hers."

The face was one Alice did not recognise either. But there was that same deep love shown in these eyes as she had seen in the eyes of the portrait that represented Jenny. This one, though, was of a man. A happy man, in his forties, who had a kindly face and was balding. And Alice knew instinctively that this was not just some casual friend. A mere acquaintance. This was a man who held something very special for the artist, and she had captured her feelings for him perfectly on paper. A picture that would be with her forever. And Alice wondered why Jenny's mother had left it behind.

Just then the door opened and Giles burst into the room. As usual, he failed to knock before he entered.

"Hey Jen," he said with a smile "Dad's just arrived home, along with Alice's Dad. They told me to come up here and send the pair of you down."

He was just about to turn and leave when he saw the sketches spread out across the bed. Instantly his attention was diverted to them and he said "What have you got there, then?"

Jenny was at a loss for words, and did not quite know how to handle the situation. On the one hand, she had never lied to Giles. And nor would she now if only he had paid heed to her in the past and treated this room as her own private sanctity. On the other hand, though, she did not want him or anyone else to know that she could draw. Alice watched her, and being such a close friend, guessed her predicament. As the two girls looked at each other, Alice made a decision.

"They belong to a friend of mine," she lied, gathering up the sketches from across the bed and returning them to the case. "I just thought I'd bring them over to show Jenny."

"I didn't know you were interested in drawing, Jen" said Giles, but not before he had caught a glimpse of the sketch depicting the balding man.

"There's a lot you don't know about me," replied Jenny and he laughed.

"Let's have a look at them, then," he said, picking up the sketch of the man, before Alice had a chance to hide it in the case. As he studied the picture closely the two girls looked on, and for a moment they thought he was going to say something. Instead, he handed it back to Alice and watched as she returned it to the case.

"That's funny," he said, looking down at the initials.

"What is?" asked Alice, closing the metal clasp.

"Those initials," he replied, pointing down at them. "A.B. The same as our Mum's before she was married. Amanda Beckworth."

He looked across at his sister.

"Isn't that right, Jen?"

She nodded in agreement.

Alice thought the time had come to close this discussion as soon as possible. So did Jenny, but she was not as bright or quick thinking as Alice.

"It's not very polite for a young man to come into a girl's bedroom with out knocking, you know." She said, in the hope that she would get some reaction from him.

"Oh, that's all right," he said, his mind distracted from the case now.

"She's only my sister. I wouldn't do it with anyone else."

"Well, you shouldn't do it with her, either. I don't allow my brother to come into my room. And I wouldn't allow you to come in either, if you were my brother."

He chuckled as he leant up against the open door.

"I wouldn't want to be your brother. Besides, I've got the best sister any body could have already, haven't I , Jen?"

The two girls smiled at each other and Jenny was pleased with his last remark. Alice, on the other hand, was a little annoyed that he had not taken the point of her argument too seriously, but there again, his mind was diverted from the art work, and that was the whole point of the exercise.

Whilst Alice gathered her overnight belongings into her vanity case, Giles continued to lean against the door and chat away amiably as Jenny remained seated on the bed. Eventually the two girls were ready to go downstairs when Giles remarked to Alice "Don't forget your drawings. Leave them here and Jen might start copying them. Aye Jen?"

Jenny felt a little awkward, but said nothing. Alice took hold of the case, the initials resting against her thigh, glanced at her friend as she passed, and walked out through the door and down the stairs to her waiting father.

# NINE

The journey back to Cirencester was pleasant enough, if not a little anxious for Alice. The case belonging to Jenny was lying on the dickey seat behind her, secreted beneath her blue woollen coat, and she prayed that her father would not notice it when the time came for the pair to climb out of the car, once they reached home.

The journey of some twenty miles took less than an hour, although Harry would normally have driven his new toy faster had he been alone in the car. But never with one of his family aboard, especially his little angel, Alice. She meant more to him than life itself. And although he bestowed many presents and finery upon her, she had never become spoilt, which was more to do with her mother's parental control than Harry's, although he would never agree to that.

As they approached Cirencester, the outline of Sheencroft House could be seen way off in the distance, elevated on a hill that rose above the town. The sight gave Harry a great sense of pride, knowing that he owned the house, and the surrounding farm. Six months ago he had bought the lot; lock, stock and barrel. Through years of sheer hard graft, a lot of luck, and a few shady, but never dishonest, deals. And it made him smile. Another ten minutes of driving and they were close enough to see the honey coloured limestone rocks that made up the bulk of the house. Large square windows, that looked dark and empty from this distance, broke up the walls, but he knew, only too well, that love and kindness dominated their interior.

Pulling into a gateway on the side of the main road leading into Cirencester, he parked up, switch off the engine and gave his daughter a kiss on the cheek. Placing an arm around her shoulder, a solid arm that had lifted many a stook of hay in its time, he smiled, leant back and sighed.

"Well? What d'you think of it, lass?" He asked, thinking that he was happier with the world right now than he had a right to be.

Alice turned and faced her father.

"Dad, nearly every time we get here you ask me the same question. And I give you the same answer."

She smiled and snuggled her head into his shoulder.

"D'you think you'll ever get used to it?"

"No, I don't think so," he said. "And to tell the truth, I hope I never do. That place up there, the house, the buildings, the land and the trees, is all I've ever dreamed of. I used look up at it as a kid whenever I came to Cirencester with my dad, and to the races at Cheltenham when I was older. I swore I would own it one day. And now I do. And no one will ever take it away."

Taking a large Havana cigar from his inside pocket he lit it and watched the smoke drift slowly on the breeze, out towards Sheencroft Farm, and disappear..

Without turning to his daughter, he said "That's ours, lass. The whole lot. Every single acre. And no one will ever take it away, not while I'm alive. That there," he waved, "is your inheritance. Yours and your brother's. And when I'm gone, you make sure the pair of you look after it. I know you will, but I'm not so sure about him,"

Alice pulled away from his shoulder with a surprised look on her face, her dark locks of hair blowing across her face.

"But Dad, I'm your daughter. The farm always goes to the son."

He turned and looked at her with such love and affection, he almost cried.

"So it does, lass. So it does. But there's more to you than meets the eye. I know that, and so will you in time. I know what you could be capable of."

He paused a moment, turned towards Sheencroft, and as he started up the Morris Cowley's engine he said, without turning to Alice "We'll have to see, wont we. We'll just have to wait and see."

# TEN

Jenny returned to the drudgery of running a farmhouse now that Alice had gone, and the men folk hinted that they were ready for their dinner. Being Sunday, they expected a decent roast, and already she was behind with her tasks. Having Alice around made her forget the drab life she led and added some sparkle to it. Unfortunately, time passed all too quickly when her friend stayed the night, and already she was aware from the grunts and groans of Jacob and her father that they were growing impatient.

"How long's our grub going to be?" asked Garnett, shifting in his old leather chair to a more comfortable position.

"My belly's rumbling."

And it showed. He was leaning backwards, his legs outstretched, and his stockinged feet near the cooking range for warmth. This caused his belly to rise and fall more than usual. The dark leather belt he always wore, measuring some two inches wide, held together by a metal buckle in the centre of his girth, held the lower half of his stomach in tight, but that in turn allowed the excess to roll above the belt. Jenny glanced towards him in disgust as she stood at the sink peeling potatoes. A wisp of blond hair trailed over her left eye and she brushed it to one side, she wondered when last she saw a more repulsive sight.

"What you looking at, girl?" he snarled, as his back caused him pain. For a moment she almost scowled at him, but did not dare and turned back to the potatoes, for there was still a few more to prepare.

"I'm starved too," agreed Jacob, stitching a new piece of leather to the side of one of his old worn boots. "Get them two girls together, and she ends up doing bugger all."

Garnett nodded as he stared at the coals flickering through the grill beneath the range.

"You're right there, son," he agreed. "I think I'd best keep them apart for a while."

Jenny stiffened but remained silent. Whenever the two of them spoke like this she always expected the worse. And usually she wasn't that far wrong.

"That mightn't be a bad idea," agreed Jacob, grinning at his sister as she stood with bent shoulders over the Belfast sink.

"Now Harry Dawson has bought that new farm over Cirencester way and made a packet from the one he sold near Lechlade, I wouldn't be surprised if they don't start getting above themselves. And that could well rub off on our Jen."

"That's a fact," agreed Garnett, looking away from the fire and prodding his hawthorn stick at a lone piece of straw laying on the carpet in front of him.

"What d'you think, girl?"

Jenny said nothing. She continued to peel potatoes. Lifting his stick, he prodded against her side, hard enough for her to flinch.

"I'm talking to you," he said.

She turned so that she was half facing him.

"I expect you'll get me to do whatever you want me to," she said quietly. "You usually do."

There was silence in the room as they looked at Jenny, and the atmosphere could have been cut with a knife. Garnett straightened in his chair so he could be closer to her.

"Don't you smart arse me, girl" he growled. "You ain't too big for a bloody good hiding, and well you know it."

In full submission now, for fear of a beating, she said "Yes, Dad," but it was barely more than a whisper. Garnett had not heard her, and his blood was starting to boil.

Whilst Jacob looked on with a smile, his father prodded his stick, this time into her belly, and said "You hear me girl? You hear what I say?"

She nodded, said "Yes Dad, please don't hurt me" and feared the worse.

"So turn and look at me when I talk to you," he said, and she turned on his command. Because she feared him, she turned away towards Jacob, and saw the look of pure pleasure in his eyes. He was so callous, so evil; it was hard to believe they were born of the same womb.

Again Garnett prodded her, only this time it was harder and she felt the pain. And the fear. Fear of what was yet to come next... Something always came next. It was a known fact. A lunge with the stick, a swipe around the face. If it caused pain, then it was sure to come her way.

"I said for you to look at me. Not him," he snarled prodding the stick into her a fourth time, harder now than before. The pain was stronger too. Much stronger, and it caused her to lean forward.

"Look at her, Dad," laughed Jacob, having forgotten about replacing the leather on his boot. "She can't take it, can she? Not a little prodding like that."

"She sure can't son." laughed Garnett. "Not like you, aye son, when you were her age. You never minded a bit of prodding, did you?"

Jacob laughed again. "Not me. I could stand it. Probably did me a bit of good over the years."

"It did that" shouted Garnett, rising from his chair, using the table for balance. "It did that all right. Just look at you now."

Tears were already running down Jenny's face as she grabbed the point of the stick before it reached her belly again. Garnett saw her hand move and pushed harder still. The force caused her to screech out in pain as the stick reached its mark

"Please Dad," she cried. "Please. No more. I can't take no more."

"You'll take what I give you," he bellowed, lumbering closer towards the range.

"And there's more to come yet."

Jacob, like a wild animal, egged him on, and the pair of them were not unlike sharks, swarming around in a feeding frenzy.

"Go on Dad. Give it to her. Give her what she deserves."

As Garnett moved a step closer he raised the stick and brought it down across her shoulder. The pain. So intense, then her arm went numb. With her right hand she grabbed the stick and forced it away, the only act she could do to defend herself. Garnett was not expecting this and was caught off balance. His right leg lacked feeling since his accident but the movement caused him to sway to the left. Towards the range. He felt himself going. The heat of the range drawing closer as he fell towards it. Instinctively he held out his left arm to save himself, knowing he would suffer. But try as he might, the arm would not react to the signal from his mind. To pull back. And as he hit the top of the range, his left hand was the first to strike. First the pain, followed by the sizzling sound of burning flesh, and then the stink of burning flesh. And as Jacob rose to drag him off, still his body weight dragged him down, and his bare arm rested on top of the range as well as his hand, and the side of his open neck shirt, originally a black and white stripe, was now turning brown. And the screams. The agony. Sounds far greater than Jenny had ever heard coming from her own lips when he inflicted pain upon her. Unable to move, she watched as the scene began to unfold. All as if in slow motion. Her father, like a mighty bull, sliding down the front of the range, unable to pull himself away because of his great weight. And the smell. That awful stench of burning flesh, mingling with the burning cotton of his shirt. She watched too as Jacob, using all his strength, tried in vain to pull their father to safety. Away from the range. But it was all too slow. The flesh still sizzled and changed in colour from red to a sickly yellow as the fat began to burn as well. And now she, in a daze, was moving towards them. Or so she thought, but her feet would not move. Her legs were rooted to the spot. And as her brother turned and stared in her direction, pleading for her help, to save their father, and she was unable to respond. Instead, she turned towards the door. And soon she was gone, out of the house and running across the open yard. Her white cotton skirt billowing out behind her On towards the barn, there to seek solace, and share her remorse with no one but herself. Throwing herself face down amongst the hay and straw, she sobbed like she had never sobbed before. And prayed to God to forgive her for the wrong she had done.

## ELEVEN

Garnett never did recover. The burns were too severe. Jacob had not been able to pull him away from the range. His weight had been too dense. And if Jenny had helped her brother, would the outcome have been so very different. The coroner doubted it. Severe burns to the body, along with shock, were a terrible combination for the body to endure. Being a medical man himself, he agreed with the pathologist giving evidence that the victim would only have lasted an hour or two at the most, if he had been pulled from the range. And so, after hearing all of the evidence, including that from Jacob and Jenny, the coroner, in his wisdom, directed the jury to find a verdict of accidental death.

As the weeks passed, Jenny tried to rebuild her life. From one that had all the markings of a poor waif suffering at the hands of a brutal father and a sex starved brother, to one where she could gain the respect she so craved and deserved from others. The first stages were painful. Very painful, and so very slow. Jacob insisted she remain at the farm, to take care of him and his every need. Whilst Giles, although now almost a thirteen year old, wanted more and more of her affection.

"I tell you, Thomas," Mrs, Dawson would often say to her devoted husband. "It's not natural, the way those two lads go on about wanting our Jenny around them all the time. Not natural at all. Why she's almost a lady now. She'll be seventeen in a couple of months. Time she started looking out for a husband."

Harry would smile.

"And no doubt you'll be the one to find her someone, my pretty," he would laugh, as he gave her a peck on the cheek.

Tabatha would shoo him away and tell him he was a silly old fool. But deep down she knew she was right. And so did Jenny, if the truth were known. Before her father's death she was already experiencing the changes in her body. The signs of puberty. Although they came late in her life. Probably where she had been beaten down and led a sheltered, albeit a brutal life. But her breasts had formed now and some nights, as she listened to Jacob snoring in the next room to hers, she would roll over between the sheets, wrap her arms around her body, and crave for the love of a good strong man.

But all that seemed a long way off. Especially to a girl who had been downtrodden all her life and never known any difference. Why, her father had only been buried these past three months. Didn't she have a family to run and care for. Giles was her life now. He needed her love and attention. Any young lad who took a fancy to her would have to wait his turn. Family ties were stronger than any other bond. Hadn't her father taught her that.

"She'll never take a shine to me," sighed Chas, as he sat one night out in the back yard cleaning the dried dirt from his hob nailed boots. Glancing up at the

147

stars, he often wondered what destiny held in store for him. He worked hard for every penny he earned, and still he never seemed to have that little bit extra he needed to buy the things he wanted in life. His mother ruffled his shock of rich black hair and placed two green china cups of tea on the rustic table as she joined him.

"She might," replied the thin hunched woman, lowering herself into a rickety old chair nearby. Still young in years at thirty nine, she appeared double her age, with a body racked from the arthritis. It was true, life had not been kind to Martha Hanks; and most days would see her suffer in pain. But she was a country woman, who would curse quietly to herself, but never aloud for her son to hear.

Chas shook his head.

"She deserves someone better than me, Ma. She may not have a lot now, but one day I reckon she'll go far."

"What makes you say that, son?" asked his mother, taking a sip of tea from the cup and replacing it back on the table with a shaking hand.

Chas watched his mother silently and inwardly grieved for her. What was her sin in life, he wondered, that she should be struck down so young. Aware that she was waiting for an answer he turned his gaze once more to the stars.

"Just something in her face," he replied, no more able to give a more definite answer than if he had been asked to count how many stars there were surrounding the moon above. But it still sat heavy with him. And though he wished so very deeply that he could be a part of Jenny's future, he knew in his heart of hearts that it was not likely to be.

"You think a lot of her, don't you?" said his mother, interrupting his thoughts. Without looking down from the stars he nodded.

"I do, and that's a fact Ma. But she'll never be mine. I know that as sure I know I'll never amount to much in life myself."

Martha turned and placed a hand on his arm; she noticed how broad and hard were the sinews and muscles. The sign of a man not afraid of hard work.

"Don't say that, son," she whispered, only too aware of the signals. Her son had been a man prone to depressions ever since his father had committed suicide when he was a child. How she had suffered then. How they had both suffered. Not only to loose the man you love, but also to loose the father you love and respect. And then having to bear the stigma and the glances from neighbours in the town. Oh yes, she had suffered through that awful curse known as depression. And now, as she sat with her son in the back garden of the small terrace house they shared, she prayed to God it was not about to raise its ugly head once more and pour scorn and agony on her poor frail body and mind. There was only so much a woman could bear, and she felt she had coped with more than her fair share.

"It's true, though, isn't it Ma," replied Chas, shifting in his chair. "I work every hour God sends, and still I can't get ahead of myself. Either the lorry breaks down, a customer can't pay, or won't pay. And every month that damn manager at the bank is calling me in to see when I'm going to square up with him. I tell you" he snapped, "I wonder sometimes if it's all worth the effort. I really do."

He paused a moment and she watched him. His eyes drifted off into space, out there, far off to the West.

"If it wasn't for Harry Dawson up there on the hill at Sheencroft" he continued, "I reckon I would have gone under long ago. He gives me work that he could well give to others drivers. Both he and I know that, and I'm truly grateful to him."

Martha nodded.

"Harry's a good man, and that's a fact. A good friend to have in times of need."

Chas nodded and continued his gaze towards Cirencester. With the last rays of the sun setting low in the West he could make out a silhouette of the hill on which stood Sheencroft farm, and for a moment, even less than a moment, he felt bitterness and anger towards Harry Dawson and all his family. Why should one man like Harry have so much, and another man like himself have so little. Life was so unfair. Of that there was no doubt. And as he sat here now, alongside his mother whom he doted on, who was growing old before her time, he wondered, as he so often wondered when he was alone, was life really worth all the hard work and determination that it took to survive. And though his resentment for Harry disappeared almost as swiftly as it came into his mind, his thoughts about the unfairness of life did not. As the sun drifted from sight and seemed to bid then goodnight, he rose from his chair, bent over, planted a tender kiss on his mother's forehead, and whispered her "Goodnight."

As she watched her one and only son melt into the darkness as he walked through the open door into their kitchen she smiled and thought how much he reminded her of her late husband, the man she had loved and cherished for just those few brief years. To be snatched from her by that most terrible of animals known to some as depression. But known to her as hell itself.

# TWELVE

It was early morning. Jenny was seated at the parlour table enjoying her first mug of tea of the day. She always enjoyed this time. She could be alone with her thoughts; before her two brothers invaded her privacy. All she had to distract her was Dog. And he was no distraction. More of a comfort than anything else. Especially since he had taken to coming inside the house on the insistence of his mistress. Jacob was far from pleased with the arrangement, but as time was passing since their father's demise, a different relationship was forming between the brother and sister who lived at Holly Bank Farm. No longer could the ruffian ride rough shod over the girl he once treated as a waif. Now he had to pick and choose his time. Mostly when that accursed animal with the wall eye and the half ear was out of the way. And that was not very often. For the old grey lurcher had formed a certain attachment with the girl. One that anyone who loves and cares for their pet would know. Where love and respect are freely given and accepted by both. And the longer the relationship continues, then the stronger the bond will grow.

Jacob had sensed this more than once. On the first occasion, soon after their father's funeral, he had raised his hand to Jenny in anger. When they were out in the cattle yard. And though the girl winced and shied back in fear, the lurcher was there at her side in an instant, having sped from across the far side of the yard. Teeth barred, with a growl coming deep from within his chest, he squared up to Jenny's aggressor, and the red mist rising in his eyes left Jacob in no doubt that the dog would attack if he were to pursue his advance. From that moment, as man and beast faced each other with such awful anger that you could sense it in the air, Jenny knew she had a protector, and at long last, for the very first time in her life, she could finally stand up for herself against her brother. And anyone else that bothered her. So long as her beloved Dog was there by her side.

Two sharp knocks broke into Jenny's thoughts. Leaving the table with Dog by her side, she walked from the parlour, through the hall and to the front door. Turning the large metal key in its lock, she pulled back the door.

"'morning Sam," she said, greeting the local postman with a smile.

"You're early this morning."

"I am that," he replied, offering her a letter with an outstretched hand. "It's the missus's birthday today and I promised to take her for a slap up tea this afternoon at that little tea room in Lechlade. You know the one. Where your friend Gladys works."

Jenny nodded. She knew the one he meant. Although she rarely went there. Only to meet Gladys for a chat. It was far too grand for the likes of her. Besides, she wanted to finish the small talk and be gone. It was not very often she received letters, and with this one, inside a pretty coloured envelope, there was the hint of lavender, and she was desperate to find out who it came from.

Sam patted Dog on the head a couple of times and smiled as the old lurcher licked the back of his hand. He had an affinity with dogs, which was just as well being a postman, and they sensed that he was their friend. Taking hold of the handlebars he climbed aboard the old black Raleigh bicycle that was standard issue from the Post Office, and with an ungainly wobble, rode off in the direction of Buscot.

"Give Gladys my love," shouted Jenny after him, and she had to smile as he attempted to turn, wave his arm in reply and negotiate a bend all at the same time. How he never came off was a miracle, and once he was out of site Jenny hurried in doors with Dog at her heels to see who the letter was from.

Once seated at the table she opened the gummed strip of the envelope to reveal a crisp white sheet of paper inside. On the top right hand corner, embossed in gold coloured lettering, were the words "Sheencroft Farm, Cirencester. Tel: Cirencester 200."

Although Jenny was not the best of readers, she half guessed from the address and the signature below that this was from Alice and could not wait to hear her news. Fortunately, as her eyes darted this way and that across the page, picking up the odd word here and there, the door to the stairs opened and her younger brother Giles walked in.

"What have you got there then Jen?" he asked, sitting in the chair opposite.

Jenny looked up and smiled.

"It's a letter. From Alice, I think."

Reaching across the table he took hold of the letter and said "Pour me a mug of tea and I'll read it if you like."

For a moment Jenny stared at him, although he was ignoring her and glancing at the letter heading. Even her younger brother expected her to do everything for him. And although she loved him more than any other, it did annoy her that just about everyone took advantage of her. But as usual she just sighed quietly to herself. Pouring a piping hot mug of tea from the blue enamel tea pot that was well past its sale by date, and with chin cupped between her hands and elbows resting on the table, she sat excitedly waiting for her brother to begin.

"My dearest Jenny,

It must be all of six weeks since we last saw each other at your father's funeral and I miss you terribly. I hope you are coping well and getting over your grief. We've all been ever so busy here getting the farm into shape. It was a bit run down when we moved in, and Dad's still not satisfied with it. I don't think he ever will be. Why I really wrote to you, though, was to tell you that I've asked Mum if you could come over and spend a few days with us, now that the house is finally in shape. Dad and I could come and pick you up. It would be no trouble and I know we would have really great fun together. Besides which, I have a parcel here that I think belongs to you, and I think it's time I gave it back to you. Let me know as soon as you can when you can come over, and I definitely won't take No for an answer.

All my fondest love,

From Alice.

xxx"

Giles passed the letter back to Jenny and stared hard at his sister in silence. Jenny, unaware of his gaze, placed the letter back in its envelope and tucked it into the top of her blouse before rising from the table and making her way over to the range. Both siblings were quiet for very different reasons.

"You'll have to go without an egg today," she said, preparing the breakfast in a large black metal frying pan.

"Half of the hens are in moult and the others have stopped laying where that fox frightened them the other night."

Giles did not reply. After a few moments Jenny turned her head and a wisp of blond hair fell down over her left cheek. She flicked her head as she so often did to remove it.

"And what's the matter with you?" she asked, knowing only too well that her brother was upset about something.

"Nothing," he replied, staring down into his mug of tea.

Turning back to the range she said "So we're in for a sulk today, are we."

"No," replied Giles. "I never sulk."

"Hmp," she grunted. "Not much you don't."

For a while neither of them spoke and Jenny resumed cooking the breakfast. She knew from past experience that she had to handle Giles just about right when he got into a strop. Not that he ever seemed too much when their father was alive. He was probably too scared to try. But now he could be a real pain, and it was this sort of atmosphere she could well do without.

Finally the breakfast was cooked and Jenny dished the fry up onto three blue and white plates that had been handed down through a number of generations. Carrying two of the plates to the table she pushed one in front of Giles and the other to the head of the table. Returning to the range for her own breakfast she said "Go and give Jacob a shout, will you. He'll only moan if his gets cold."

Giles did not move, and began cutting into a large lump of fried bread, piled high with bacon, tomatoes and fried potatoes left over from the previous day.

"Did you hear what I said?" Jenny asked, pulling up her own chair and patting dog on the head as he rolled over and lay down beside her.

Giles said nothing.

"I won't tell you again, Giles," she said, showing that she was a little annoyed.

He swallowed a mouthful of bacon and said "So what will you do if I don't call him."

Jenny held her empty knife and fork up in her hands as she glared at her brother, and leaned forward across the table.

"I'm telling you for the last time. Either you go and call him, or you're asking for trouble."

She knew deep down there was little she could do if he refused, for he had grown into a strong lad, although far short of Jacob. But still he would have been a handful. And any form of violence against him she would never tolerate if she could help it. But since their father died, she was slowly asserting a form of authority over her younger brother that was having an effect on him. She was no longer the poor little sister that he could walk all over. She was starting to lay down her own set of rules. And whilst Jacob would never adhere to them, Giles knew that to enjoy the type of life he treasured when he and his sister were alone, then he must abide by these rules. However much it meant that he must give in. But having said that, there were times like with any youngster, he would try and kick against the traces, and Jenny's patience would be tried to the limit. But fortunately, up until now she had always come out on top.

"Giles," she screamed, with such force that both brother and dog jumped up together and stared at her.

"Do as you're told. Now!!!"

Giles knew he had pushed her too far and scurried off up the stairs and out of sight like a bolting rabbit. Any sulking that may have been in his mind had dissolved and would have to wait for another day. Leaning over the side of the table Jenny stroked Dog's head to calm him and smiled as she offered him a small piece of bacon rind.

"That'll teach the little monkey," she chuckled as Dog looked up for more. "I'll show him whose mistress of this house, and that's for sure."

## THIRTEEN

Days passed, and although Giles sulked occasionally, where he disliked the idea of his sister leaving him alone with Jacob at Holly Bank Farm, Jenny ignored him whenever he played up. She merely busied herself with chores about the farm, and wondered how Jacob would cope without her. Milking the cows was one occupation he loathed. Mainly because he thought cows were vicious animals, who would flick their tails across his face out of spite when he was sat down against their flank squeezing at their teats. And on many occasion he had been kicked across the cowshed, along with a milk pail, or out through the door. Yet this had never happened to his sister, who had a certain rapport with animals, and again this was something neither sibling had in common.

One afternoon, when she caught Giles in a good mood, after returning home from school, she talked him into writing a letter for her confirming to Alice that she would be pleased to stay with her for a few days. It had been a hard decision, one that had plagued her for a number of days. What with Giles sulking and throwing the odd tantrum; and Jacob becoming a real pig to live with. And occasionally threatening to become quite violent whenever they discussed the matter. But being brought back to his senses as Dog appeared as if from nowhere and squared up to him. But finally the decision was made. She knew that if ever she were to grow into a mature woman, with a life of her own, then she must take a stand and let her siblings and others see that she was not a push over. She had a will of her own. Albeit that it had been lost in the past. In fact, never really developed. But she was now determined that, come what may, she would make the effort to alter her life, and run it the way she wanted. Not as others thought she should.

And so it was that the big day arrived. A day that was to mark a milestone in the life of Jenny Couling. Where she was about to start on a journey that would change her life, and that of those around her.

As usual, she rose early and cooked breakfast for her brothers. Giles was the first down, followed shortly by Jacob, who slumped down into the chair that used to be occupied by his father, but which now he considered to be his own. Watching Jenny, standing with her back to him at the range, in her new pink and white cotton dress, that hugged tight around her waist, he felt movements in his groin that were hard to control. Giles, as usual, was engrossed in a book and never noticed the look of lust on his older brother's face.

"You're definitely off, then?" asked Jacob, watching every movement Jenny made as she swayed from side to side preparing the meal.

She nodded and simply said "Yes."

The last thing she wanted right now was to get involved in an argument. There had been too much of that in her life in the past. Already her stomach was tensing up though. The knot was there; the butterflies were creeping around.

Her breathing was short and sharp. She just wanted for the next couple of hours to pass swiftly. To hear the sound of Harry Dawson's car pulling up outside, to leap in alongside Alice and know that she was safe for the next few days. That she could relax. Enjoy herself. Surely she was entitled to that. A little bit of happiness was everyone's right. And if she didn't weaken now, then she may experience it for herself

The meal was cooked. Two plates piled high, ready to be served. And a third, half the size, which was hers. She only had to turn and cross the room. It was not difficult. Anyone could do it. Anyone, that is, bar Jenny. Even from here she could feel the eyes of her brother, piercing deep into her back. That horrible, controlling feeling; that made her feel sick to the stomach. One she had experience many times over the years. That she had done something wrong. It was all her fault. He had the power to control her. Why, oh why did he do this to her. Why did he have so much power over her?

No. Not this time. This was the one occasion where she was going to make a stand. She took a deep breath, filled her chest and pulled her stomach in. With head held high she turned and, with all three plates balanced on her arms, she looked straight ahead and crossed the room. Still aware that Jacob watched her, every step of the way. And though she could not see them, she sensed his eyes had that strange look deep within, which she had seen so many times before; but which she did not understand. To her, still a virgin, and not wise to the world, it

162

was a mystery. To Jacob, it was something else. Pure unadulterated carnal lust. Something which he had tried hard in the past to control, but which still, whenever he saw Jenny in a certain pose, would raise its ugly head again. And as he watched her cross the room towards him, knowing he would not be seeing her for a number of days, he experienced another feeling which was completely alien to him.

At first, as she drew nearer, hips swaying involuntarily from side to side, he could not understand what it meant. He knew it was wrong to lust after her. All form of religious teaching, all rules laid down by mankind; they all screamed out that it was wrong. And time after time he had tried to control it. God, how he had tried. But he was not strong enough. He was only a man. It would need something or someone far stronger than him to subdue these feelings. And now she was nearly upon him. With that long soft blond hair, the wisp hanging down, as it so often did, down the left side of her face. And those pale blue eyes. The eyes of innocence. Eyes that were not looking at him, but were aware of him. Almost unseeing. Yet so full of life when she laughed.

As time seemed to stand still for the pair of them, he gradually understood the new feeling he was experiencing. As she stood near him, bending over, to lower the plate onto the table, he could smell the sweetness of her body, coming through her clothes, the merest hint of rose petal oil on the air. And he knew, in that instant, that this new feeling had come as a way to save him. For if they had been left alone when she looked like this, smelt like this, he would have been unable to control himself. He would have committed that most awful of carnal sins. He would have ravished his own sister. That he could not have lived with. Not knowing that he had committed such a terrible sin; and having to remember that for the rest of his life. And because of that knowledge, he was pleased to accept the feeling of relief that washed over him, the feeling that had suddenly come upon him. Almost washed him clean. To know that his sister would not be his temptress for a few days was like the breaking of a new dawn.

# DARK   SECRETS

## PART   THREE

### ONE

Jenny enjoyed her time with Alice at Sheencroft Farm. Five days of pure bliss. The weather was in her favour, even though the last heat of the summer sun was beginning to wane. But there was still enough warmth left to walk the fields with her friend, wearing no more than a flimsy dress, coloured white and summer blue. Her blonde hair flowing loose about her back, almost reaching down to her waist. And they would laugh together; at little things. Some that were fun, some that hinted of embarrassment. Such things that young ladies, showing the first signs of maturity, would discuss as they began to develop. As they began to grow.

Each morning she was allowed to lay in, until a maid called her down to breakfast at eight o'clock. Something she had never experienced before. Silk sheets, spread neat and taught, across a large double bed that she was allowed to occupy herself. Where she could slowly prize the sheets apart at night, slide gently and tantalizingly into the gap between, and loose herself within the folds.

Pull them tight around her; feel the softness against her body, as she pulled her old faded night dress from above her head, fully intending to cover herself again before the morning came. To make herself respectable once more. Yet always waking that little bit too late to make it worth the while.

All this and more was slowly making Jenny realise that she was indeed a young woman. Not some silly child, who had no say of her own. Here, at Sheencroft, with such palatial surroundings, with servants to wait upon her every need, and her friend Alice to model herself upon. She knew, in her heart of hearts, that this was what she wanted. This was the type of life she so desperately needed to aspire to. To throw off the shackles of her past.. The drudgery, the heartache, the pain. To let the world see that she was indeed a young woman. According to Alice, a very beautiful woman. Although she had yet to see that for herself... She still felt that she was the ugly duckling. The one that no one looked at. But who knows. One day. It happened before; where an ugly duckling turned into a beautiful swan. So maybe that was yet to come.

With one day left to enjoy the pleasures of the farm, the two girls were strolling arm in arm across the lawn at the front of the big house. It was mid morning and the sun was rising high in the sky, casting shorter shadows now than at any other time of the day.

Alice turned to her friend and said "You're looking sad today, Jenny. Is anything wrong?"

The older of the two girls by a few months stared off into the distance before making a reply.

"I think I'm confused more than sad," she said finally.

"How do you mean?" asked Alice, turning to her somewhat surprised.

"Haven't you enjoyed yourself while you've been here?"

"Oh Alice, it's not that. Of course I've enjoyed myself," she said, pulling her friend closer with a tightening of her arm.

"I can't think of a time when I've been happier."

"So what is it then?" Asked Alice.

Jenny shook her head and smiled.

"I just don't know. I wish I did. I'm so confused about life in general."

She paused.

"How do you mean?" asked Alice.

Jenny sighed.

"I think it's being here with you these last few days. It's opened my eyes to what life can really be like. Not like it has been for me these past few years. Cooking and scrubbing for the boys. And for Dad when he was alive. Here, with you; with your Mum and Dad, and Samuel, life is so different. You all treat me like an adult. In fact Samuel treats me like a real lady sometimes."

Alice laughed.

"I told you he'd taken a shine to you."

Jenny blushed, but said no more about Alice's older brother.

"No, but I'm being serious," she said as they continued their walk across the lawn towards the long graveled driveway. "Living here with you and your family this last week has really made me realise what life can be like."

Alice nodded.

"I know what you mean. I'm really grateful for what we've got here. And I know Mum and Dad have worked really hard so that Samuel and I will benefit from it. But, like Dad says, if you want something bad enough and you work hard enough at it, then you can achieve anything in this world that you want to."

Jenny wasn't too sure about that.

"It doesn't always work that way," she said. "I've always tried to work hard and do what's right by everyone, and I don't seemed to have achieved much."

Alice chuckled.

"That might be because you haven't tried hard enough at the right things."

"How do you mean?" asked Jenny, just a little bit surprised.

"Well," replied Alice. "Take your paintings. You..."

"Yes," butted in Jenny. "I was really annoyed when you showed Peter my folder. I told you right from the start that I didn't want anyone to see them. And what do you do. The very first person that comes along and you go and show him every one. And Mum's as well. She'd be furious if she ever found out."

Alice was undaunted. In her mind she had done the right thing by her friend.

True, it was slightly underhand. And maybe she should have asked Jenny first. But she knew what the answer would have been. So when her father informed the family that he was inviting a few friends over for an evening meal last night, and that one of them would be Peter Laughton, a local art dealer from Cheltenham, who would give Harry some advise on the type of paintings that would both suite the decor of his home, and also be a worthwhile investment, Alice approached her Mother immediately. True to her word, Tabatha arranged the seating plan for Alice to be next to Mr. Laughton, and Jenny sitting opposite him. Not that Jenny had the slightest inclination as to Alice's plans. In fact, no one had. Not even Tabatha. All she knew was that her daughter felt Mr. Laughton, being a relatively young man in his early thirties, could easily become bored with the older company that evening, and the two girls could add some sparkle to the conversation. Tabatha had to admit she could see no harm in this, and unwittingly, went along with the plan.

"I did it for the right reasons," said Alice, trying to hide a smile.

"That's not the point," snapped Jenny.

"They were mine. My own private paintings. I'd painted them in private, and that's how I wanted them to stay. Just mine and Mum's."

She paused to catch her breath and Alice was quite surprised at the outburst.

"Look, I'm sorry," said Alice. "I know you got a bit upset last night, but I thought you could see how it could help you. And I thought it was all over now."

"That's just it," snapped Jenny again. "It's always what you think. Not what anyone else thinks. Just you. It's always you. You thought it would be a good idea if Peter saw my drawings. You thought he could sell them for a lot of money. And yes, maybe he can. At least he thinks he can. But that's not the point. How do you know what I think? How do you know whether I want to sell them? Have you ever thought of that?"

"Of course you want to sell them," replied Alice. "What other reason would you have drawn them for if it wasn't to sell them? That's what all artists draw for, isn't it?"

"Is it?" Asked Jenny. "Is it really. How do you know? Have you ever asked any?"

"Well, no," said Alice after a pause. "But that's not the point."

"Of course it's the point. Don't you realise. Can't you get it through your stupid thick head? The last thing I thought about when I was drawing them was that I wanted to sell them. The money. I wasn't drawing for the money. I was drawing them for pleasure. Because I was out in the fields. At one with the countryside. It was pure; wonderful pleasure. Money never came into it. And it was probably the same for Mum. And now look what you've done. Shown them to Peter. In no time at all, if what he says is true, they could be hanging in his gallery for all the world to see and people will come along and buy them. And

I'll loose them for ever."

"But if that's what you felt, why didn't you say something about it last night. At the meal. When everyone was talking about them." asked Alice.

"Because I'm not like you," said Jenny, staring away off into the distance.

"I'm shy. I'm unsure of myself. I could never have stood up in front of all those people like you did last night, and say I didn't want anyone to see them. How could I. I would have looked such a fool. So I just had to go along with it. Just like you had arranged."

Alice stopped and turned to her friend.

"Look Jen," she said, taking hold of her hand." I didn't realise. Honestly I didn't. If I had done, then I would never have done what I did."

Jenny looked at her but remained silent.

"I really did think it was for the best. Honest. I thought all along they were wonderful drawings. And when Peter said they were some of the best he had seen for a long time, well. I just felt so pleased for you."

"Did you really," asked Jenny.

"Of course I did."

Jenny gave the merest hint of a smile.

"Well, it's over and done with now, I suppose. There's nothing I can do about it. We'll just have to wait and see what happens, wont we."

Alice pulled Jenny towards her and they embraced.

"I'm truly sorry, Jen. Honest I am. The last thing I would want to do is spoil our friendship. I care too much for you ever to allow that to happen."

Jenny smiled as the tears welled up into her eyes. Brushing the side of her face against Alice she nodded.

"Me too," she whispered.

# TWO

Giles looked up from stroking Dog on the hearth. The two had formed a certain bond since Jenny had been away. And although Giles had never been particularly close to the animal, he sensed the old feller was missing Jenny, and comforted him whenever the notion came to him.

"You're looking smart tonight," he said to his brother, who was searching the parlour after spending the best part of an hour sprucing himself up in his bedroom.

"You going somewhere?"

Jacob did not reply at first. Instead he asked if Giles had seen the key for the old Austin Seven they kept parked in the yard outside. It could hardly be called a car, for it was more an old battered rust bucket. But it served its purpose. And after the pick up was written off at the time of their late father's accident along the Lechlade to Fairford road, "The Mustard Pot", as Austin Sevens were affectionately known in those times, would have to do.

Giles told him the key was hidden behind the mirror that rested upon the mantle shelf above the cooking range.

"What's it doing there?" snapped Jacob, as he crossed the room and kicked Dog out of his way, causing the animal to yelp and scurry off into a far corner of the room.

"You shouldn't do that" retorted Giles, following the old animal and placing his arms around the dog's neck. "He'll bite you back one of these days, you see if he doesn't."

Jacob laughed as he found the key and smoothed his hair down in front of the mirror.

"I'd just like to see him try."

But in truth, he knew the day may come. For he had seen on more than one occasions when the fancy had taken him, that he would threaten Jenny and the old dog would bare his teeth in protection and the red mist would rise in his eyes. And that he thought strange. For, during the past week, whilst Jenny had been visiting her friend, Dog had shown no sign aggression towards Jacob. In fact, every time Jacob had come near him, when Giles was not stroking him or making a fuss, the dog would scurry away like a coward towards a corner, or off out into the yard. But whenever Jenny was around, he was like her protector. And that did not please Jacob.

"Damn animal should never be in here. All flea ridden and mangy like he is."

"He is not," snapped Giles. "I've cleaned and brushed him every day this past week. Just like Jenny told me. So you can't say anything is wrong with him."

"He should never be in here," snarled Jacob, grabbing his old brown leather jacket and pushing his arms into the sleeves.

"If I had my way, he'd be out there every night where he belongs."

And deep down he cursed his sister. For it was she who had brought the damn thing in every night in the first place; and now, if he did try to leave it outside, like he did the first night she was gone, all it would do is howl for hour after hour and keep him awake. That he could not put up with, and although he felt like putting a bullet through its head, he thought the aggravation he would receive from his sister, with all the tears and the sniveling, was hardly worth his while. So in the end he decided, against his better judgment, to let the animal sleep in the house, so long as Giles take care of it and kept it out of his way. That was when Giles and Dog first forged their bond, and no doubt, now it had formed, it would last for the remainder of Dog's life.

"I'll be back late." he snapped, walking out and slamming the back door behind him.

Giles knelt down and lay against Dog.

"I wish Jenny was back" he whispered, stroking the long hair around the animal's neck.

"Still, only one more night. She'll be back home tomorrow."

As if he understood the boy, Dog licked his arm, and soon both dog and boy were sound asleep on the parlour floor.

# THREE

"Keep still," smiled Jenny.

"How do you ever expect me to finish this tonight if you keep fidgeting?"

"Sorry," replied Alice.

"But it is very difficult to stay still in one position for any length of time. You ought to try it sometime."

Jenny laughed.

"I'm the artist. Not the model."

"That's true." replied Alice, trying desperately hard to remain still now that she had been reprimanded.

"And one with a very fine future, if what I've heard is true."

Jenny paused to sharpen her pencil.

"And just what have you been up to now?" she asked, leaning forward so the pencil shavings would fall into the small wooden box she used on the kidney shaped dressing table, and not onto the beige and brown bedroom carpet.

"Oh, nothing," replied Alice with a smile

"I don't believe you." said Jenny.

"You've definitely been up to something."

"No I haven't," replied Alice, wondering whether she had said too much already, especially after this mornings little episode out on the lawn, where

Jenny had given her a piece of her mind. But she was the sort of girl who always had to be doing something exciting. It was just in her nature. A part of her make up. Jenny placed the sharpened pencil back on the table, sat bolt upright and folded her arms.

"What are you doing?" asked Alice in surprise.

"Until you tell me what you've been up to, I'm not going to draw another line. So if you want your portrait finished, then you tell me. If you don't, then don't bother, and I'll rip it up right here and now. The choice is yours."

Alice looked at her friend with a new sort of respect. Never had she heard her make a demand like this, and although, after the initial shock, and realizing that she was, or may be, joking, she had to admire her for making the stance. The silence was clearly audible in the room as the two friends stared at each other. Alice looking prim and proper in a brand new lace dress, coloured royal blue with white trimmings, just for this occasion. Jenny, on the other hand, in a plain but comfortable white shift, which, although not stylish, made her appear as attractive, if not more so, than her friend, sitting on a polished mahogany chair opposite.

"Well," said Jenny, after a pause.

"What is it to be?"

For possibly the first time in her life, Alice knew she had met her match. Although a pleasant girl, like so many girls of her age, she was vain. She liked to make herself look beautiful, and in return for her effort she liked other people to see that she was beautiful. So she had asked Jenny to draw her portrait; because she knew her friend was a very talented artist. And now, at the crucial time, when she knew the portrait must almost be complete, Jenny was threatening to tear it up into little pieces. The very thought was almost too much to comprehend.

"All right," she exclaimed, as Jenny moved forward with a glint in her eye, threatening to take up the portrait from the table with two hands and do her worst.

"I'll tell you."

Alice pulled her chair closer to Jenny and smiled.

"I took a telephone call this afternoon," said Alice.

"It wasn't actually for you, but it was about you. The caller said they wanted to keep it a secret until they called round tomorrow and saw you personally. They were phoning just to make sure you would still be here."

Jenny looked both curious and surprised.

"Who was it from?" she asked, becoming more than a little excited. She was not used to receiving telephone calls; especially ones where the caller wanted to meet her personally. And the fact that Alice had kept it a secret so long seemed to have little relevance. She was far more interested to know who it was that wanted to speak to her.

"Well, I shouldn't really tell you. Not until tomorrow, at least."

"Tomorrow," repeated Jenny.

"Why tomorrow?"

Alice smiled, determined to drag this out as long as possible.

"Because someone thinks you're a very clever girl, and they want to tell you so to your face."

Jenny shifted forward in her chair.

"What on earth are you on about, Alice. This just isn't making any sense."

Glancing at the portrait, now almost complete, laying on the nearby table, she placed her hand on it.

"I'm warning you." she said, trying to sound as though she meant it.

"If you don't tell me right now what this is all about, I'm going to carry out my threat and that will be the end of it."

Unable to reach far enough forward to grab the drawing and bring it to safety, Alice had to concede.

"All right," she said, "But first you've got to promise me that you won't tell him I told you."

"Him," exclaimed Jenny, now even more excited, and more than a little intrigued.

"That's right," replied Alice.

"Him. But first I want you to promise."

"Yes, yes. Of course I promise," said Jenny, barely able to contain herself.

"Well," continued Alice, slowly and deliberately...

"Peter Laughton is calling round to see you tomorrow"

Jenny clasped her hands to her lips and took a sharp intake of breath.

"Peter Laughton," she said, in barely more than a whisper.

"Peter Laughton, the art dealer. Coming here to see me."

Alice smiled, and was genuinely pleased for her friend.

"That's right," nodded Alice.

"You met him last night, remember. At the meal."

"Of course I remember him," replied Jenny, almost in a daze.

"I'm not likely to forget him, am I?"

Alice chuckled and shook her head.

"I don't think so. He took rather a shine to you, didn't he?"

The mere thought made Jenny blush.

"Don't be silly. Of course he didn't. What would he see in someone like me?"

"A lot more than you think he does," smiled Alice.

Jenny thought about last night. And she thought about Peter Laughton too. A tall, handsome man, aged 32 years, according to Alice, who had gleaned the information from her father. Well built, but lean, with a strong rugged face. Dark wavy hair, swept back and clear blue eyes that were the first thing she noticed about him when he entered the hallway after being introduced by

William, the butler. They were eyes that smiled as the two of them were introduced, and as he took her hand, she felt so much power surging through his grasp that she felt slightly weak at the knees. As they were shown to their places at the long dining table, he seemed more than pleased that they were seated opposite each other, and as the evening progressed, he appeared to monopolize any conversation with her. Not that she disapproved. In fact, after the initial shyness had worn off, she began to enjoy his company, and was more than a little surprised how swiftly the time had passed when the meal finally came to an end and the men retired to the drawing room to indulge in their tobacco and port. In fact, she was somewhat bored being back in the company of women. But she was even more surprised, when, at the end of the evening, when all the guests began to leave, that Peter Laughton actually took the trouble to find her. Taking her hand in his, he slowly drew it to his lips, and with all the confidence of a man who knew she would not withdraw, placed a gentle kiss on the back of her hand and bade her goodnight. She was left stunned and speechless, and her eyes followed him as he strode resolutely through the hallway and out through the main door, bidding other guests goodnight with a cursory wave of his hand.

Still leaning forward in her chair she looked at Alice.

"So, what is he coming to see me for?" she asked, more than a little excited at the prospect of seeing him again.

"You must tell me. It's too much to expect me to wait until tomorrow to find

181

out."

Alice shook her head and moved her chair back to where it was before Jenny threatened to tear up the portrait.

"I can't do that," she said with a smile, as she adjusted her body and clothing, so it was back to where it had been before they started this conversation.

"You know I would if I could. But he did make me promise."

She smiled again and paused for a few moments.

"And you know as well as I do that it's wrong to break a promise. You wouldn't want me to do that, would you?"

Of course Jenny wouldn't, and her friend knew it only too well. That was why she had said it that way. She wasn't her best friend for nothing. She knew her strong points, but she knew her weaknesses as well. And she knew that Jenny would not expect her to break a promise, whatever the circumstances. So the up and coming artist just shrugged her shoulders, took up the pencil and tried to continue the drawing, knowing only too well that she would have to wait until the following day before she could find out this secret that interested her so much. But she was sure it would all be worth the wait in the end.

# FOUR

Whether it was the sound of the back door being slammed too, Dog stirring, or whatever, Giles wasn't sure. But already he was awake. He knew something was up. His brother was in a foul mood as he staggered across the room towards the table. The electric light had not been turned on and Giles could barely see him in the half light that filtered through the windows, as a full moon drifted slowly back and forth behind wispy clouds as they continued their endless journey across an open sky.

"Why you still down here?" snarled Jacob, his words still slurred from the effects of alcohol, his arms steadying his body against the table.

"You been sleeping on the floor with that mutt again?"

Giles knew from experience it was best to remain silent. One wrong word, one sentence delivered so that it caused offence, and the true wrath of his brother could be brought down upon him in a second; or upon the animal he had grown to care for, almost as much as his sister.

In the half light he could just make out the side of his brother's face. A large face, with short cropped hair, and eyes that stared vacantly out of the window on the far side of the room. In the half light, as Jacob shifted his stance where he felt weak, the light from a distant moon showed up four uneven scratches running the length of his face; all the way down the left cheek. From above the temple, down nearly to his chin. Blood had congealed around them, but not so dry and dark that Giles did not know they were still recent. Maybe within the last hour. An hour and a half at the most.

"You hurt, Jacob?" he asked, in a voice that, through fear and uncertainty, was barely more than a whisper. Jacob breathed deeply and steadied himself, taking in great gulps of air.

"Hurt," he laughed, with an air of madness in his voice.

"You think a tart could hurt me."

He almost fell. But grabbed the side of the table just in time, steadied himself and brought himself back, almost to his full height. Giles was shocked. He turned away. When he saw the scratches, he never for one moment imagined they were caused by a woman. Jacob was always in scraps. Nearly every time he went out. So Giles just assumed another man had ripped open Jacob's face. Not a woman. Surely not. As Jacob gasped for breath, all manner of thoughts ran through Gile's head. Wild, crazy, ugly thoughts. Those borne of a young immature thirteen year old's mind. A boy having barely reached puberty. Of a young well developed woman, being thrown to the ground. Clothes ripped from her body. Her firm rounded breast now bare, her naked thighs being forced apart, revealing a dark mound of hair that should remain pure and untouched, waiting for the man she loved.

As he turned and stared at his brother he felt nothing but revulsion. He felt sick to the stomach. Here was a man he was supposed to look up to. A big man whom he should respect; and who should, in return, respect him. Yet those scratches down his face, gouged deep by the nails of a woman, must surely show that this was someone who nobody could respect. An animal. In fact, worse than an animal. In the animal kingdom the male of the species would often force himself upon the female. Had he not seen this often with the large bulls and the boars around the farm? Climbing onto far smaller and weaker females. At times forcing themselves onto the females. There to create their progeny. But that was the difference. The act of mating there was to create life. To ensure the survival of the species. Not like this. Not like Jacob. Forcing himself upon a female. Just for his pleasure. That was all wrong. So very wrong.

Jacob beckoned with one hand.

"Come here," he grunted.

Giles stared at him in the half light coming through the window, but refused to move. The very sight of his brother, and what he must have done, appalled him.

"Come here," repeated Jacob again, his voice more sinister than before.

Giles's body grew tense with fear. His stomach tightened. His breathing was short and shallow. He feared the worst. Dog, sensing the atmosphere in the room, pulled himself from the floor, ambled over to his favourite corner, where he knew he would be relatively safe, and flopped down again. Giles on the other hand felt far from safe. He now felt entirely alone.

"You hear me boy," shouted Jacob impatiently.

"Get over here, like I tell you."

Giles knew he must obey. Or run. But if he ran, the day of reckoning would come soon enough, and he would receive a beating. There was little choice. Slowly, his eyes watching Jacob, like a mouse watching a cat, he moved forward. The distance was not great, but it seemed like miles. Already he could smell the stench of beer, mixed with stale sweat, radiating from his brother's body. And it made him feel sick.

Once the young boy was close enough, Jacob threw an arm around his neck, allowing the full weight of his body to fall upon the young boy's shoulders. Giles's legs buckled, but he straightened up before he reached the floor, and somehow made his way to the stairway. After a marathon climb, with Jacob sometimes clinging hold of the banister, at other times letting it go, he reached the top of the stairs. With one Herculean effort, he threw his brother onto the bed, and, with no thought given to removing his boots or jacket, walked out, closing the door gently behind him. With a long deep sigh, he returned to the parlour, with new and strange thoughts clouding his mind. He was pleased by Dog's company, and together they sat, side by side on the floor, staring into an empty fire. The animal was in a world of his own. With Giles, there was the fear of a new dawn, and what was yet to come.

# FIVE

Morning was a long time coming for Jenny too. But for a very different reason than that of her brother. The thought and excitement of seeing Peter Laughton before she left Sheencroft had kept her awake most of the night, and now, with a new day dawning, she was eager to be up. Yet she also desperately wished that time would slow down. Almost stand still. For, though she desperately wanted to see Peter. To talk to him, to smile, to allow him to take her hand in his, maybe even to give her the lightest of kisses on the cheek  She also dreaded the time when he would say his final good bye. For she knew, deep in her heart, that once she had seen him today, and they had finished their business, whatever that may be, she would not see him again. How could she. They moved in such very different circles. Him, a high powered art dealer with contacts all around the world. Her, a mere country girl, who rarely left the farm. No, of course not. There was no way their paths would ever cross again. They would be strangers once more.

And so it was, as these thoughts were rushing through her mind, that she became aware of a knocking on the door and one of the housemaids asking if she could enter.

"Of course," replied Jenny, clawing herself back to reality and raising herself up onto silk covered pillow cases.

"It's just past eight o'clock, miss," smiled the maid sheepishly as she scurried around, pulling back the long velvet curtains, and placing a fresh white hand towel next to the wash basin. Jenny watched silently from the bed, and realised how much this girl reminded her of herself. They were both of the same age, within a few months. They were of the same stature. And both walked with a slight stoop. This was not caused by any deformity or impediment, merely that they felt subservient to those around them. In their own company, or in the company of those of a similar class, they would walk normally. In some case, almost upright. But it was always there, like some great yoke on their back. Always pulling them down.

Obviously this maid felt inferior to Jenny, and she wondered why. They were probably from a similar background, lacked a decent education, and would no doubt remain in gainful employment for the remainder of their lives. So why should one feel inferior and the other not.

As Jenny's eyes followed the maid around the room she slowly began to realise that background and education had very little to do with the difference she was experiencing. Age neither. If one had been older than the other, Jenny imagined the class structure between the two would have altered very little. The more she thought, the more it slowly dawned on her. Background, education and age had nothing to do with this at all. It was what the maid had perceived.

Her position in life was a maid. Probably a very lowly one. She was employed to take care of Jenny, and seeing that Jenny was a guest of her employers, she perceived that Jenny was of an equal standing to her employers. Far above the status of a poor working maid. The fact that Jenny spoke in a broad Gloucestershire accent had nothing to do with it. The maid had perceived Jenny to be of a higher class status than herself, and so long as Jenny did not disclose the fact that they were both more or less equal, the maid would be none the wiser.

As she was left alone once more to dress and prepare to join the family for breakfast downstairs, she suddenly realised that, whenever she felt ill at ease or uncomfortable with people around her, she would only have to recall this time, early one morning at Sheencroft Farm, when a maid entered her room. When she realised for the first time in her life, that she, Jenny Couling, could achieve anything she wanted. Merely by allowing people to believe that she was something special. Whether she believed it or not was immaterial. Just so long as they believed, that  was all that mattered. If she could achieve that with other people, then she would succeed.

Breakfast was picked at, rather than eaten by Jenny that morning, and on more than one occasion, Tabatha Dawson inquired if all was well with her daughter's friend. Jenny explained that she was fine, just a little disappointed that the visit was almost over, which in part was the truth. However, when Tabatha suggested that the whole family would be more than pleased to see her again as soon as the fancy took her, Jenny gave a genuine smile, saying that she would make arrangements with Alice in a few weeks time. Thankfully the course of conversation soon changed from Jenny's welfare, and it did not seem long before everyone had finished and were preparing to leave the table.

"Not long now," smiled Alice, leading Jenny out across the lawn towards the stables at the rear of the main house.

"Not long for what?" asked Jenny, with a cheeky smile that would never have crossed her lips a few weeks ago.

"As if you need ask," replied Alice, opening the main wooden gate leading into the yard. Once Jenny was through, she closed it securely behind them, and as the two girls, dressed in slacks and loose fitting blouses, walked towards the stables, they received many an admiring glance from both groom and carter alike.

" 'Mornin' Miss Alice."

The head groom greeted Alice with a customary nod and dipped his cap.

"Will it be Starbuck today?"

Alice viewed the horses as the majority peered out through the top sections of their stable doors and agreed that she would. He was a tall black stallion and had to be her favourite. Apart from herself and one of the more experienced grooms, no one else was able to ride him. Jenny, on the other hand, settled for a much more docile animal. A gelding by the name of Dancer. It was hardly an appropriate name; for he was well into his sixteenth year, and had to be coaxed ever get him to move. But his disposition, which was quiet and gentle, suited Jenny, and she loved his colour, a light golden bay, with three of his four fetlocks coloured white.

This had been one of Jenny's favourite pastimes at Sheencroft. Coming to the stables each morning and riding out. Thanking the groom, who gave her a leg up into the saddle, she had to smile to herself whenever Alice mentioned the words "Riding Out." It sounded so very grand. Just like they were part of high society. Which of course, they were not. And never would be. Although Alice liked to think that she was almost there.

"You've improved a great deal since you've been here," said Alice, pulling sharply on Starbuck's reins as he tried in vain to canter across the yard where he was full of high spirits.

"Do you think so?" asked Jenny, leaning forward over Dancer's withers, urging him to walk on.

Alice could not reply. She was far too busy keeping Starbuck under control. With another flick of his tail he would turn first this way, then that. Give a small buck in the air. Snort and pull on the reins. And he would only settle when the two horses and two girls were out through the gate and cantering across the open twenty acre meadow. As usual, Jenny was some way behind Alice and her stallion, but it did bother her. She rode for pleasure. She loved to feel the wind

in her hair, the freshness on her face, and the gentle movement of the horse

beneath her. Before her visit to Sheencroft she had not ridden for many years.

Probably not since she was eleven or twelve. She knew it had to be before her

Mother walked out. Before then she owned a small New Forest pony. A little

white mare with a short cropped main. Very much like a zebra's mane. A lovely

little thing that she was very fond of. But when her Mother left, her father

became really annoyed, and out of sheer spite, sold the pony one day, so that

when Jenny returned home from school, she found it had gone. He never did tell

her what happened to it. She remembered she cried a lot for many days. But she

had learnt how to ride well on that pony, and it stood her in good stead now.

 As she watched Alice from a distance, she was sure she was riding too fast.

Dancer had only managed to canter half way across the field, but already Alice

and Starbuck had reached the far side and were now veering off on a tangent to

the left, where Jenny knew there was a fast flowing brook, dividing this field

from the one beyond. She tried to call, but all was in vain. The distance was too

great, and the wind was blowing towards her, away from Alice. If she had heard .

the calls, knowing Alice as she did, Jenny doubted if she would have taken that

much notice. And she was probably right. So instead, she pressed Dancer into

what can only be described as a moderately fast canter or a slow gallop, and

together, as they veered off to the left, they slowly closed the gap between

Starbuck and her friend.

Jenny had never been an envious person. It was not in her nature. But she certainly envied Alice that day. To see a horsewoman control an animal like that, an eight year old black stallion, sleek and in his prime, was something to behold. The strength and nerve required. To make him gallop at such speed, and still have the confidence to know that you can control him, to make him bend to your every need, was something she would remember for the rest of her days. And not just by the use of the reins and the hands; and the crop. But the whole of your body. The twisting and turning, the leaning this way and that in the saddle. The use of the calves on his flanks. To grip the animal firmly between your inner thighs. To make him bend to your every command. Your body above his, so he knows that you are the mistress. That you dominate him at all times. That he is yours. And yet still, he is a free spirit, with a will of his own.

That was the moment when Jenny believed she made a conscious effort to change her life. Having seen it was possible for a woman, a slight woman like Alice, to control a mighty animal like Starbuck, made her realise that it had to be possible for her to tame the beast that shaped her life. Those that made her shy, self conscious, and afraid. The time had come when Jenny Couling would change into the woman she rightly deserved to be. A woman that people would respect.

# SIX

As arranged the previous day, Peter Laughton arrived at Sheencroft Farm at eleven am sharp. Dressed in a black three piece suite, white shirt and black tie, he appeared every part the city gent. He always dressed in style and the twenty two carat gold ring, set with sixteen rubies and four diamonds, resting on his right hand, showed that he was a man of wealth. As with all things, he knew that, to warrant admiration, class should not be overdone. The ring proved this. The diamonds sparkled and shone in the sunlight, and the rubies complemented the more expensive stones. It was neither gaudy nor ostentatious. A small plain signet ring with his initials rested on the fifth finger, and apart from a pair of eighteen carat gold cufflinks, that was the sum total of jewelry he wore that day. The maroon jaguar purred along the gravel driveway, passing gardeners along the way, and as he pulled up alongside the thirteen stone steps leading up to the main house, he saw Harry Dawson, standing at the top of the steps in front of the dark oak door.

Harry, unlike his guest, possessed no dress sense whatsoever. In all his forty eight years he had never yet managed to master the art of refinement. And though his wife Tabatha had tried her best, she had virtually given up on him over the past few years.

To see Harry standing in front of the open door, wearing an extremely loud

194

yellow, brown and orange check three piece suit, brown boots, and sporting a large Havana  cigar, was not unlike watching Toad of Toad Hall welcoming guests to his humble abode in that well know film, Wind in the Willows. Harry was portly, round and often red in the face. But to anyone meeting him for the first time, with that constant smile upon his lips, would think he had not a care in the world.

"Welcome, me boy," he shouted, offering Peter Laughton an outstretched hand, which was accepted, as the younger man reached the top of the steps in a few short strides.

"Nice to see you back so soon again."

Peter smiled and followed him through the hallway.

"Does Jenny know my reason for coming?" he asked, as Harry guided him through the doorway to the drawing room, and waved towards one of the leather bound chairs, well known for their comfort.

"I believe she knows your coming. From what I can make out, Alice let the cat out of the bag last night."

Peter looked disappointed, but Harry soon put him at ease with a smile and a decent sized glass of sherry.

"But she doesn't know why you're here. In fact, none of us know that."

Harry lowered himself into one of the vacant chairs, oblivious to the sound of air escaping from between the leather and the wooden frame. Peter smiled.

195

"Not for much longer, Harry. I promise you" he said, savoring the flavour of one of his favourite Sherries, a very fine Bristol Cream.

"D'you want me to get her in here now?" asked Harry, leaning back, after he had knocked ash from his cigar into an oversized green onyx ashtray that lay on the floor alongside his chair. He enjoyed the trappings that came with wealth, and it showed.

"I'd sooner have the whole of the family in here, if that's ok with you," replied Peter, studying the various paintings around the room, and thinking that, without prompting, Harry had made the perfect choice in deciding which room Peter would explain the reason for his visit.

"No problem," answered Harry, reaching over and pulling on a brass bell pull that protruded from the wall.

"Wonderful things, these are," he said with a smile.

"Don't know how we'd manage without them in a place this size."

Peter nodded in agreement. He liked Harry and he knew he wasn't bragging about his wealth, as some people would in his position. In fact he liked and respected the whole of the Dawson family. But deep down, he did feel that Harry was a big likable buffoon. Not stupid by any means. No one, who could acquire a property the size and quality of Sheencroft Farm, purely by their wits and endeavours, could be classed as stupid. But for all that he tried, Harry was not, and never could be, classed as Lord of the Manor. It was just not in his make up. He was merely a good old country farmer who had made it good. That was how he was now, and how he always would be. A big, hearty, likeable rogue.

The door opened and William the butler, who was well into his sixties, entered the room.

"You rang, Sir?" he asked, giving the merest hint of a bow.

Harry smiled. He liked William. Liked the way he greeted him every morning. Delivered his papers neatly ironed, made sure his boots were always cleaned and polished daily by one of the servant boys. He liked his manner. The way he showed Harry and his family respect. True, he was probably well past retirement age. But he was already a part of the household when Harry bought Sheencroft, and in his wisdom, he had decided to keep him on. And not a bad decision it was either.

Harry explained that he would like all the family, along with Miss Jenny, to come to the drawing room as soon a possible. William nodded, said "Right away Sir," and retired.

Peter had noticed the relationship between the two men, and wondered just how William regarded his employer. This was a man who had obviously served and waited on persons of high esteem. A trait you could never lay at Harry Dawson's feet. Yet he showed his employer great respect, and probably realised, soon after the arrival of the Dawson clan at Sheencroft Farm, that if he played his cards right, here was a meal ticket for life.

Not long after, the door opened again, and Tabatha entered, followed by the two girls, now changed from their riding habits, into more presentable frocks. Peter rose to his feet and was greeted by each in turn. Soon, they were all seated, with Jenny occupying the chair directly opposite Peter, with Alice a little off to her left, and Tabatha alongside her husband.

"Well," wheezed Tabatha, once she had shuffled around in the chair and made herself comfortable.

"This is all very exciting, I must say."

Peter rose to his feet for the second time since the women entered the room.

"I'm sorry I've been so secretive about this," he said, with a smile on his face.

"But I have some news which I think might interest all of you, and make the wait worth while."

Placing his right hand into his inside breast pocket he withdrew a plain white envelope and turned to Jenny.

"This, young lady," he said, pausing for a moment, before handing it to her, "is for you, I believe."

All eyes in the room turned to Jenny as she cautiously took the envelope in her hand.

"For me?" she said, staring down at it with uncertainty.

"That's right," replied Peter, standing above her, with hands pushed deep into his jacket pockets.

"And if you'd like to open it now, we can all see what's inside."

For a moment Jenny's hands trembled, and although she was amongst friends, she still felt terribly insecure. The whole situation seemed very surreal. As if she was not really here. Eventually, with shaking hands, she withdrew a letter from inside, and as she opened it, a cheque fell from within the folds and landed on her lap.

"What does it say?" asked Alice excitedly, leaning towards her friend.

Jenny, knowing she would have difficulty in reading the letter, passed it to Alice as she examined the cheque. Who it was from, she could not be sure. Or for how much. But she recognised her name as the payee.

Always the impatient one, Alice began to read.

"Dear Miss Couling,

Having visited Mr. Laughton's gallery today, I was most taken by your work, especially the four sketches of the garden birds. Being a collector and somewhat of a connoisseur on wild life sketches myself, I knew I must have them the moment I saw them. I have asked Mr., Laughton to inform me the moment he receives more of your work, and look forward to purchasing more sketches from you in the future.

Yours faithfully,

Isabella Woolstrome."

Alice handed the letter back to Jenny and almost snatched the cheque from her grasp.

"How much has she paid you?" she asked, barely able to contain her excitement.

"Really, Alice," reprimanded her Mother.

"That's no way for a lady to behave. Give Jenny back her cheque this instance."

Fortunately for Jenny, Alice was far too excited and pleased for her friend to take much heed of her Mother right now, and before anyone could utter another word she was already reading the cheque.

"My golly," she gasped aloud. "She's paid you fifteen guineas."

"What," gasped Harry, barely able to believe his daughter's words. Leaning forward, he beckoned with his hand, and took the cheque that Alice passed to him.

"She's right, you know," he said, his eyes scanning the piece of paper before him. "Fifteen guineas. Fifteen guineas for four drawings."

He turned to Jenny and beamed a great broad smile.

"That can't be bad, girl. Can it. I reckon you're on your way to fame and fortune, aye."

"I don't know about that, Mr. Dawson" said Jenny, beaming as much as Harry as he returned the cheque.

"But it is exciting, isn't it."

"Exciting," roared Harry. "I'll say it's exciting. In fact, I think it calls for drinks all round, don't you?"

"Isn't it a little early in the day for drinks, dear?" asked Tabatha, who realised she was wasting her time, as Harry was already up on his feet and pouring more drinks from the cut glass decanter that contained the Bristol Cream Sherry. Once everyone had a glass in their hand, including Jenny, who was unaccustomed to alcohol, he raised his own glass in the air and proposed a toast.

"Here's to a very special girl," he said, with a smile that showed he was almost as proud of Jenny as he was his own daughter.

"A good girl, an honest girl, and a really fine artist."

Everyone agreed and joined in the toast. As they returned to their seats, only Peter remained standing. Placing his empty glass on the side table he raised his hand to his mouth and gave a slight cough.

"There's just one more thing I'd like to add," he said, turning once more to Jenny.

"I think you ought to know, Jenny, that Isabella Woolstrome is one of the best known art critics in London. She's respected by everyone who is anyone in the art world, and if she says a piece of artwork is good, then you can believe it is. And so will everyone else."

Jenny stared up at Peter in disbelief. Was she really hearing this? Or was it all some fantastic dream. Peter continued in a very somber voice and everyone in the room remained silent.

"I really do think you ought to take your art seriously. Both Issabella and I think you have a great future. If your work is managed and displayed correctly, then within a year or two, you could become a much sought after artist."

He paused, allowing the enormity of what he had said, to sink into the mind of this poor timid country girl. He knew she must not be rushed. If he wanted to manage her, then he must gain her trust. Slowly, gently. Handled correctly, she could make him a fortune. He waited until the time was right. When she looked up at him, into his eyes. Unsure what the future held. In a room surrounded by friends, where she was completely alone. He alone could show her the way. And now the time was right.

"I'm not sure if you're aware, Jenny, but I'm agent to some of the top selling artists around the world. I sell paintings for them, and they make thousands of guineas. I could name them, but that would be irrelevant. You're the artist we're discussing right now."

He paused again, his eyes never leaving those of the young girl before him, but constantly aware that everyone in the room was watching and listening to him. He was the center of attention now. Just how he needed it to be.

He continued.

"You do realise that you have a choice."

She continued staring up at him, and spoke quietly.

"I do?"

He nodded.

"A very simple choice. Either, you can return to your farm. Carry on with your day to day life. Tending to the livestock, taking care of your brothers, draw the occasional sketch that will never be seen by anyone. Or there is the other alternative"

He paused again but she said nothing. She just looked up into his eyes.

"You could find yourself an agent. A good one. One who had the right contacts? Could exhibit your work around the country. Maybe around the world, if you were good enough. You could make a fortune. The world could become your oyster. You could do exactly as you pleased. No one would rule your life. You would be mistress of your own destiny."

And that was it. He had said enough. Now she was completely unsure as to which route to take. She desperately needed a crutch to lean on. Someone to guide her through this whole new world that she could experience. Where she could sketch, draw, paint. The very things she loved, more than anything else in the world. Had he not said the world could be her oyster? She could be mistress of her own destiny. Yes. That was the life she wanted. Had she not thought, over the past days, weeks even, that her life could become something so much better? Not the poor quiet country girl. With a farm to run, a pig of a brother to live with. To care for. Here it was. In her grasp. Here for the taking. He was offering her everything she had ever wanted. The freedom, the happiness. And all she had to do was say yes.

"Think about it, Jenny," he said, breaking into her thoughts.

"And if there is any way I can help, then just let me know."

# SEVEN

Peter Laughton bade the Dawson's farewell, leaving Jenny in a daze. Meanwhile, not a hundred miles away, her brother Jacob was in a daze too. But this was one of his own making. He woke late, leaving Giles to tend the animals before he left for school, and as he turned over in his bed to taste the tea left by his younger brother earlier, he realised it was cold. Falling back onto the pillow, still more asleep than awake, he felt pain down the side of his face. Slowly, as he felt the weals with his finger, thoughts from the night before drifted back into his mind. The evening had started well. A night in The Nags Head was always good for a laugh. That was where he met his cronies. Other country boys, who lived in nearby hamlets, or on local farms. Beer was swallowed by the gallon, and cheese and onion sandwiches were supplied, at a price, to soak it up. The trouble was now, though, that many of his friends had married, and as time passed, fewer and fewer would turn out for a pint at their favourite pub. True, some were under the thumb, and had to obey the little lady. Or large lady, as was often the case. Others would stay away, for fear of being denied their nuptial rights on their return from a night of heavy drinking. And then there were those who just got plain fed up with the boozing life, decided to start a family, and ended up with a hoard of kids running around that had to be clothed and fed. Jacob was not one of these, and did not intend to become one. He had a great deal more he wanted to get out of life than end up being married with a string of kids following him around. But he still had his carnal desires.

And that was where the problem lay. There were many a young lady, or tart as he would call them, who lived around Buscot, Lechlade and the surrounding area. All in their prime, and ready for servicing. But the problem was, none of them seemed to fancy him. Oh sure, they would laugh and smile, flirt with him a little, and cause the passion to rise in his loins. But that was where it always stopped. Just at that point where he was about to perform his duty. And if ever a situation could rile a man, then that was it. Excitement turned to frustration; passion turned to hate. Or at least, with Jacob this seemed to be the case.

Take for instance, the tart last night. Had he not been good to her? Spent a fortune on drinks. And not your ordinary pint. Oh no, he had splashed out on the best. Spirits. Vodkas, gin. You name it. Whatever she asked for, he supplied it. True, it may have been to his advantage. Get her pissed, and he could have his wicked way with her. And wasn't that what it was all about. All through the evening she had appeared up for it. Laughing at his jokes, stroking the inside of his thighs. Kissing the back of his neck. And when he had suggested they go for a drive in his Austin Seven and find a more secluded spot, she didn't say no. So what made her change her mind at the last minute? To try and stop him making his advances. God, the more he tried to understand women, the less he could.

She was still in his thoughts when the sound of the back parlour door slamming shut brought him back to reality with a start. He knew from the late summer sun, shining through his bedroom window, that it must be somewhere around mid day. Giles would be at school. He was not due home 'till three thirty or there abouts. As he listened, he realised there was no sound from Dog. Although the mutt was pretty useless, he did have one saving grace. He was a good guard dog, and would let you know in plenty of time if any unwanted visitors were about. So it must be someone he knew.

Slowly, as his brain began to clear, he realised it was Monday. The first day of a working week. At first he could draw no significance from that fact. Should it mean something special? He didn't think so. But already he could pick up the sounds of someone moving around downstairs.

Pulling himself from the bed he searched for his boots, only to realise that he was still wearing them. He cursed his younger brother for not taking the trouble to undress him the night before. God, he felt rough. Which surprised him. Normally, after a skin full the night before, any sign of a hangover would have cleared by this hour. Grabbing a great lump of beech wood he always had laying by the side of his bed, just for this purpose, he slowly made his way down the stairs.

Whoever was in the house was coming from the front room, back into the parlour, and would, in a few seconds, have to pass by the door leading up to the stairs. He waited a few moments, swung open the door, and with the beech wood held high above his shoulder, showed himself to the intruder. Jenny leapt back in shock, almost stumbling over Dog, who was following a short distance behind.

"Jacob!" she gasped, clutching her hands to her chest.

"What on earth are you doing here?"

"I happen to live here," he growled, lowering the lump of wood to his side as he brushed past her and ambled over to the table.

"More to the point, what are you doing here?  Coming back at this time of day."

"It's Monday," she replied, in a tone he wasn't used to.

"I told you I'd be back today. I wasn't sure of the time, because Mr. Dawson had to fit in whenever he could to drive me over. As he was on his way to Buscot about some business, this was the time that suited him, and it suited me too."

Taking the beech wood from the table, she placed it against the back door and, after letting Dog out so he could have a good run around, she looked around the room before adding "And now I suppose I'd better get started and clear this place up, seeing you and your brother have made it look like a pig sty."

Jacob turned in surprise.

"Don't you go getting saucy with me, girl." he said, in a tone that would normally have turned her legs to jelly.

"If I choose to live like this, then I'll live like this. And there's nothing you can do about it. You understand."

She knew something like this would happen, ever since she left Sheencroft Farm. And she was prepared for it. Whether she could pull it off was another matter. But at least she would try.

Crossing the room, she stood above him, and stared down into his eyes. With his face turned slightly to the left away from her, and his eyes turned to the right, staring up into hers, she had yet to see the marks to his cheek.

"Now you listen to me, Jacob Couling," she snapped, her arms folded across her chest, causing her breasts to heave in and out in time to her breathing.

"You may be a bully, and known as a hard man locally. And you may think you can order me around just as you please. But you don't scare me any more. You hear."

For a moment Jacob remained silent, trying to understand the change that had taken place in his sister. Normally she was so quiet and docile. Would hardly say boo to a goose. Yet now, she was trying to rule the roost. And he had to admit to himself that he liked it. A woman with spirit always excited him. But he was not about to let on. Not yet, anyway.

"So I don't scare you, aye?" he said, turning his face slowly towards her.

Jumping back in horror as she saw the full state of his injuries, she cupped her hands to her mouth as she gasped aloud.

"Jacob," she said in barely more than a whisper. "What on earth has happened to you?"

Leaning back in his chair he forced the cotton material between the buttons of his shirt to pull apart, exposing some of his beer belly.

"That, my girl," he said, with a sneer across his face, "is none of your damn business."

"And guess what?" he added, almost as an afterthought.

"What?" asked Jenny, having lost her composure completely.

Leaning forward and standing up to his full height, he towered over his sister and stared down at her. A thought had just come into his mind.

"If anyone should ask who did this to me," he said, pointing to the scars running down his face, "Then I'll be telling them it was you."

"Me!" Shrieked Jenny.

"What are you talking about? Why on earth should I say it was me?"

"Because," he snarled, grabbing her by the throat, with a large rough unwashed hand, "if you don't, then I'll make sure you live to regret it."

Feeling the hand tighten around her throat she began to cough and wheeze and a real sense of fear filled her small, slight body.

"Jacob, please" she gasped. "Let go. I can't breath."

Jacob smiled, with that awful evil smile that she had come to dread over the years.

Giving one final sharp squeeze that caused her to jump involuntary, he finally eased the pressure before pushing his face up close against hers. She could smell the stale beer about his body. The old tobacco smoke on his clothes from the night before in the pub, although he did not smoke himself. And the stench of his breath. It made her feel sick. And all the nightmares over the past number of years came flooding back. Nothing had changed. Nothing ever would change. It was all some great dream that God had instilled into her mind, that would never come to fruition. She was as downtrodden and afraid now as she always had been, and in her heart of hearts, she knew it would never change.

"So, you agree, then?" he said, with such menace and venom that she dare not disagree.

"Yes. Yes, if that's what you want." she said.

"Yes, I'll say I did it."

As the two drew apart she rubbed her neck to ease the pain and stared down at the old tiled floor, too afraid to look him the eye.

"But what reason can I give if anyone asks. Why would I have done it to you?"

By now he had reached the back door. As he opened it, Dog trotted in, and now that Jenny had returned, the old lurcher hardly gave Jacob a second glance as he crossed the room to be at his mistress's side.

"Tell them we had a row. You can think of something. You lost your temper, and before I realised it, you had rushed me and scratched me like this. Just make them believe it, that's all."

Walking through the door, he turned once more, stared at the dog, before turning to her and said "Make sure you keep that mutt in here. Along with yourself. I've got things to do outside, and I don't want you two pestering me.

Slamming the door as he left, Jenny wondered what he meant. There was little chance of Dog leaving her side now she was home, and even less chance of her joining Jacob outside. The more she thought about it, the more she wondered what he had to hide.

After heating the kettle on the range, and pouring herself a mug of tea, she returned to the table, where she was joined by Dog. Lowering herself into the chair, tears welling in her eyes, she patted her faithful companion on the head and then took a sip of the hot sweet tea. Taking a deep breath, she looked across the room at the far wall, and gave a deep long sigh.

"Oh Dog," she whispered.

"What am I going to do? Is there no end to this? Am I never going to free myself of Jacob and his accursed temper?"

Dog licked her hand, as if he understood her plight, before he too gave a great low sigh, and settled down by her feet.

Jenny thought long and hard. So much had happened over the past week. She had spent most of her time with Alice over at Sheencroft. And it had been happy times. They had laughed and joked, and enjoyed themselves, just as young ladies should do. She had ridden again, like she did when she was a young child. She had learnt that she was a competent artist, something she would never have dreamed of before she met Peter Laughton. Peter. Now there was a man. Tall, suave, handsome and sophisticated. Not like any man she knew around here, or had ever known before. Certainly not like Jacob. He was a pig of a man. A downright slob. And then there was Chas. Poor old Chas. But would she give him a second glance now. True, he was a kind and trusted friend. And at one time she had probably felt more than just a fondness for him. When her father had been involved in the accident with the truck across the Lechlade to Fairford road. Then she needed the support of a true friend. And he had supplied it. Free of charge. No question of receiving anything in return. It was there on offer all the time. But that was then. This was now. Another man had entered her life. A man who could offer her everything she had ever dreamed of. Or so he had said.

Why oh why could she not take up the challenge. Every time she thought she was about to change her life in some way for the better, something had to come along that brought it all tumbling down again around her heels.

She slammed her fist on the table with such force that even Dog jumped from his resting place. Such action was completely out of character for her, but she was annoyed. Annoyed with people. Annoyed with life itself. And she felt slightly better for the small meaningful outburst.

213

Leaning forward after a few moments had passed, she settled Dog down with a stroke of her hand and returned to her thoughts.

Here she was again. In the same position that she had been in so many times before. Stuck. Unable to go anywhere. Just because of her brother Jacob. Whatever was going on? Why on earth would he insist that she lie to anyone that asked, and say that she had caused those scratches down the side of his face? And why would he insist that she did not venture outside. It didn't make sense. There must be something he had to hide. There just had to be. No other explanation could be found for his behaviour. The more she thought about it, the more curious she became.

Telling Dog to stay, she finally plucked up the courage, and, as if Jacob was already watching her, crept towards the back door. Closing it behind her, she looked around to see if there was any sign of her brother in the immediate vicinity. All seemed quiet. There was no sign of him in the small garden she tended out back, which consisted mainly of herbs. Odd flowers had been placed at various places around the low sandstone walls, which gave more interest, and honesty, with its mauve flowers and leaves that looked liked pennies in a purse, was in keeping with her nature. Along with the honesty were the occasional groups of hollyhocks, giving height where it was needed. And her favorites were the sweet peas. Large plants, interwoven amongst the bamboo stakes, or crawling up through amongst the fennel and dill. Such delicate colours, ranging from the soft whites, pinks and yellows to the stronger blues, reds and crimsons. Regularly she would snip off the flower heads once they had gone over, thereby encouraging more growth and flowers, rather than allowing the plants to go to seed.

Now she was creeping along the cobbled path that she and Giles had lain some years back; turning in two gradual curves, before reaching the small wrought iron gate, now open and standing between a pair of four foot pillars of sandstone.

In the yard she stopped, her eyes darting left and right, ever watchful, lest she catch sight of her brother. The dominant cockerel, resplendent in his reddish brown plumage, chased a small white hen across the open yard towards one of the two barns that lay off to the right, divided by the cowshed that stood between them. The hen, squawking as she fled, disappeared into the larger of the two barns, the cock not far behind her.

Jenny was running all manner of thoughts through her mind as she desperately tried to think of an excuse should Jacob catch sight of her. Which of course was rather a waste of time. If he saw here, there would be no need for an excuse. What would be the point? She would have gone against his orders, and of course, she would then suffer the consequences. How she wished that Dog was by her side. She would have felt safe then. Jacob would never have dared touch her. But that would have defeated the object of her task. The whole idea was to remain secret and silent. Dog would have ruined that.

But already Dog was inside the parlour, desperately trying to chew himself a way out through the door. It was as if he knew his mistress was in possible danger. And he was desperate to be by her side.

She had two choices. Turn to the left or to the right. For some reason she decided on the left. Why, she could not explain. There was no reason for it. It was a choice and she had made it. Half crouching, half running, she crossed past the open slatted wooden gate that led out onto the main road, then breathed a sigh of relief as she reached the block of buildings that had at one time served as stables, but now, thanks to Jacob, lay derelict.

The first entrance she could see, as she peered around the corner, was a double stable door painted green, and the upper half was open. Easing forward, always looking towards the barns on the opposite side of the yard, she reached the door and went to slide the bolt. It was stiff, and hard for her small delicate hands. But she needed to be inside. Out of site of Jacob, should he appear suddenly from anywhere around the yard. After a great deal of heaving and shoving it was finally free and she was inside. Pulling the lower half of the door too she breathed a sigh of relief, and for a moment, wondered just what she was doing. Was this really the actions of a young lady. An accomplished artist who had sold four drawings. And, received the mighty sum of fifteen guineas to prove it.

As she thought of the money, she was glad she had taken Mr. Dawson's offer to change the cheque into cash from his own pocket, and all she had to do was sign the back. She didn't really understand what that meant or proved, but she trusted Alice's father like he was her own, and any time he gave advice, she would usually take it.

Breathing heavily, she was suddenly aware of a knocking sound coming from one of the barns across the way. Which one it was she could not be sure. It may even have been coming from the cow shed. After all, the three buildings were all joined together. First she heard three knocks. Then silence for about thirty seconds. Then she heard it again. From the apparent safety of the stables, she peered around the corner of the open door section, eager to find out where the sound was coming from.

Again there was silence, apart from the deep lowing of a cow in one of the nearby fields. Instinctively she knew it was Beth. A big old Friesian, with one horn missing, and barely a short curved stump for the other. She had calved the day before Jenny left for Sheencroft. She would now be calling for her calf, locked away in the cow shed for the day, so she could produce milk enough for the family. The calf would have his fair share after she had been milked. It may seem a cruel way to treat a young calf, only a few days old, but that was the way of country folk. If the calf had been left running with his mother all day, there would have been little enough milk left by milking time. And that was not the

217

way to run a farm.

Unsure whether to make a move, Jenny decided to wait a while. To cross the yard, with nowhere to hide, would be sheer folly. Yet make a move she must. One way or the other. She could not stay here all day. After all, she was the one who had made the decision to come out and find out what Jacob was up to. Either she must pursue her original course of action, or just give up and return once more to the house.

Fortunately, as happens in so many cases where fate takes a hand, the decision was made for her. Having stepped back into the relative safety of the stables while she was making up her mind, she now peered out from the door again, and was surprised how dark it had become outside. She was just in time to see Jacob striding across the yard towards the farm house. He appeared hot and sweaty, as though he had been excerpting himself, which made her all the more curious as to what he had been up to.

Suddenly, and without warning, a mighty thunderclap burst across the darkening sky. The sound was so loud and intense, lasting for a good five to ten seconds, that Jenny was forced to cover her ears with her hands. Never had she heard thunder like this before. And so sudden. No sign of lightning to herald its coming. It was there for a few seconds and then gone. And now the rain. At first, only a few drops. Splattering onto the concrete yard. Dark uneven spots, contrasting with the surrounding light colours of the yard. Slowly they increased, both in size and intensity, and soon they were hammering down onto the corrugated tin roof of the stables, so much so that Jenny was almost deafened by the sound they made.

Eager to make her move, she looked out again, and was aware how dark it had now become. No sign of the sun. That was far up and behind the dark awesome clouds that now covered the land. She felt strange. Almost afraid. Who was she fooling? She was afraid. She wished she wasn't, but she was. As the clouds brought darkness, almost like an eclipse that she had experienced in the past, that very darkness almost brought her comfort. For as she ran across the yard, an old hessian sack held above her head giving some form of protection from the rain, she knew that Jacob would still be indoors. She doubted he would venture out again until this storm had cleared.

Reaching the cowshed, she rushed in and slammed the door behind her, throwing the sack to one side. Leaning against the uneven whitewashed stone wall, she breathed deeply, her lungs heaving in and out and she felt the cold rain water trickling down her neck, onto her back, and she shivered. The thin white cotton dress she wore was hardly suitable clothing for a mission such as this. Especially in this weather. Already soaked through by the torrent outside it was clinging to various parts of her body, and she was now wishing she had been carrying her shawl, which she could have used to cover her modesty.

The calf looked up through the railings from where it was laying in the pen at the far end of the shed. A small black bull calf with a white fleck to the center of its head. If she had not been away at Sheencroft for the past week, it would have probably greeted her. For she made a pointed of showing great tenderness and affection to any youngsters born on the farm. And the calf would have been no exception. But the calf remained silent. It merely stared at her out of curiosity, with soft dark tender eyes.

Deciding which barn to head for, the one to the left or the right, she crept off to the left, past the stalls where the milking cows would be tethered when she was doing the milking, and onto the dividing door that separated the cowshed from the grain barn. The door squeaked on its hinges as she pulled it forward, and she was grateful for the sound of the rain outside. Suddenly there was another mighty clap of thunder made her start. If only, she thought, she had brought Dog with her. He would have made her feel safe but he was still indoors, where she had left him. Where he could do no harm. And she knew there was little chance that Jacob would let him out, once he arrived at the house.

The barn was large. Some thirty feet by sixty. Built fifteen years earlier it was already showing signs of age. Split boards around the outside walls, the two large double doors beginning to rot away unevenly at their bases. Tiles missing from the roof at various points, allowing the rain to pour through, forming large puddles on the floor. Hard to see all this now. For it was almost dark inside, where the storm clouds outside were concealing the sun. But she remembered the inside of the barn. She had seen it all before. Many times she had played in this barn. With Giles, her brother. And sometimes Dog. And even her Mother, when she was still here. They would often chase each other around the barn, over the sheaves of corn laying on the floor, waiting for the gang of threshing men to arrive with their machines in late autumn. They had been happy times then. But everything had changed now.

For a while Jenny remained still, listening for any tail tell sound. What it would be, she had no idea. A rustle, a thud, a knock. It could be anything. She heard the sound of a mouse, running across the floor, from one side of the barn to the other. And a bird, possibly a starling, scurrying around somewhere in the rafters. But they were normal farm yard sounds. She was listening for something more. That knocking sound she heard earlier had come from somewhere in this direction, but where she could not be sure.

As she looked and listened, she became aware that the rain had stopped. A gradual silence was creeping across the yard, through the walls and on into the barn. At first it was pleasant, a relief after the earlier downpour. Now it was almost eerie, though. And she felt even more nervous. But with time this feeling slowly passed. As clouds parted so the sun began to show itself again. Streaks of sunlight filtered through gaps in the boards. Water stopped pouring through the roof. Now there was little more than a trickle from the various holes above, and many of these were turning into no more than droplets. The floor appeared a stage, the sun highlighting the more important points of interest. And Jenny appeared like a starlet, in the center of this stage, shafts of sunlight acting like spotlights picking her out as a real beauty, her white cotton dress, still clinging to the outline of her body. Her semi naked legs, moving this way and that, in her continuing search for a clue around the great barn.

Jacob watched her, secreted as he was, on the far side of the connecting door. Set back in the darkness, she could not see him, even when she turned in that direction. The darkness of the cowshed contrasted sharply with the brightness now filling the barn, and Jacob drooled as he watched her.

Slowly she turned away, the dress flowing loosely in time to the body. She crossed the barn, towards the far side, climbing over the sheaves that lay in her path. She jumped and squealed once in fright, as a farm cat, an old black Tom, scurried past her, off out into the yard, in search of who knows what.

In the far corner of the barn, small, dark and scary, where the sunlight could not reach, she saw for the first time, her worst fear. An area of the floor, measuring some five feet by three, freshly dug and patted down again, with the long handled shovel resting against the wall.

"You just couldn't leave it, could you?" he snarled.

The words brought her back with a jolt. There was no need to turn. She knew it was Jacob,. But turn, she did. In the half light of the barn he looked fearsome.

Like some beast of prey, about to kill its quarry. The only light reaching the corner of the barn fell on the left side of his face, exposing the scars from the night before; and on the right side of her body, exposing the outline of her hips, the outline of her breasts. His eyes studied her; the whole of her. And he became excited. He felt the blood rushing to his groin.

The pure white dress, still soaked from the rain, clung tightly to her in places, loosely in others. As he watched her, small whiffs of steam caused from the heat of her body drifted upwards into the air; barley visible, save where the light shone through the barn.

Jenny was scared. Probably more so than at any other time in her life. Jacob was acting the animal. One could say, he was the animal. The look in his eyes was enough to tell. He was looking at her, he needed her, he wanted her. And she knew it. Not until now did she really understand. Before, when he had looked at her, fondled her, she had never been sure. Never quite understood what he wanted. She knew it was wrong. That was obvious. But again, why it was wrong she had never been sure. If she were older, more worldly like other girls of her age, then of course she would have known. But she had always been a quiet country girl. Living out in the country side, alone with her father and two brothers. No one had ever discussed the ways of men and women. How they acted towards each other. The difference between a couple who loved each other, and a couple where the male purely lusts after the female. She had never been taught that. But now, here, alone in this barn, she was being taught the raw, unadulterated truth first hand. And it scared her. How she wished she was not here all alone.

Already Jacob was moving towards her. Like a lion stalking its prey. Slowly, one footstep at a time. Barely making a sound. God, how she needed help. How she needed someone to come and save her. Anyone. She began to shout. A small feeble shout at first. A shout so feeble that even if there had been anyone in the yard outside, they would probably not have heard her.

Jacob smiled. A narrow, evil smile.

"That wont do you any good, girl," he whispered.

"Not now. Your mine. You're all mine."

She was backing away, one step at a time. And all the while he was moving towards her.

She screamed again. Louder this time. But still no one heard her.

Her legs were trembling as she moved farther back. Her right foot caught something. Something hard. It was one of the boards sticking out from the wall. And now her back struck the wall and she felt faint. There was no where else to go.

Jacob's breathing was heavy now. His eyes were bright with lust and desire. She noticed a swelling in the crotch of his trousers, and prayed to God he would leave her alone. But still he kept moving towards her. Closer and closer. And

224

again she could smell the stench of his body. And she felt sick. Her stomach tightened and she began to wretch.

"For God's sake, Jacob," she whispered, as she took a deep breath.

"You can't do this. Not to me. It isn't right."

He merely laughed, and already he was grabbing her. Around the shoulders at first, pushing himself onto her She felt the bulge between his legs pushing hard against her. She twisted this way and that. Trying so hard to free herself. But it was all to no avail. He had wanted her for so long, and now the moment had come. All thoughts of guilt left him. Lust and desire conquered guilt and sanity. She was here now, and he was going to have her.

The next ten minutes or so were no more than a blur. A mixture of fear, panic, shame and pain. In which order they came she could not tell. She remembered certain things. The most graphic. She remembered he ripped her dress apart, from the top, right down to her waist, where she would not yield to him. She remembered how he threw her to the ground with such force that the wind was knocked from her body, so she could not breathe for a while. And she remembered at some stage, she clawed his face and her finger nails struck home. For there was the sign of blood. But whether it was his or hers, she did not know. It was on her hands, and across her dress. Down the front of her dress. He also held her to the ground and forced her thighs apart. Of that she was sure. What happened after that, though, she could not remember. Whether she passed out or her mind refused to accept what happened, she never knew.

At the end of it, she was aware that he was lying on top of her. The whole of his body. Covering hers. Like some dead weight. It seemed strange. One minute he had been forcing himself on her, like a man possessed. Unable to control years of pent up desire. She had been screaming and using every ounce of strength she could muster to keep him off. The next, he was still. No more writhing, no pushing, no fighting. He was now a dead weight. He breathed out one long great sigh, shuddered, and then the full weight of his body was resting upon her. Crushing her into the ground.

# EIGHT

She entered the parlour by the back door and turned the key in the lock. Dog greeted her like an old lost friend, but she ignored him. Pulling her dress around her semi naked body, she pulled the bath tub from the out house and began to fill it with hot steaming water from the kettle off the range. Tears welled in her eyes, but she was determined not to cry. Not yet, anyway. Once in the tub, she scrubbed her body hard, with a brush and carbolic soap. Down her front, round her hips, between her thighs. Working up a lather with the soap between her hands, she rubbed her breasts, her face and rubbed the soap into her hair. Every part of her body was soaped and still she did not feel clean. So she emptied the water down the drain and repeated the process, and still she felt dirty. She felt she would never feel pure and clean again.

Pouring the last of the water down the drain again, she dried herself off with a large soft towel, wrapped it around her and after pouring a strong sweet cup of tea, sat down in one of the arm chairs next to the range, and thought of what had gone on over the past hour or so.

Why oh why did she decide to go out there into the yard in the first place. It was a stupid thing to do. Of course Jacob would find her. He was bound to. Even if not out in the yard, then when he came back into the house. He would have realised she was missing, and come after her. And wasn't that what he had done. Come after her. Groped her like some wild animal. Defiled her. Ruined the rest of her life.

That thought annoyed her, and already anger was coming to play its part. Why should someone like him have the power to have such an effect on her? Why should he, just to satisfy his lustful desires, be able to ruin her young life in just a few short minutes? As she sat there, staring into an open fire place, thoughts were already racing through her mind. Not weak, pathetic thoughts as she might have expected, having just been abused and defiled in such a manner. But strong thoughts. Thoughts of hate, of revenge. She knew she could just sit there and feel sorry for herself. Allow him to take control again, the moment he walked back through that door. But that was the easy way. And she had had enough of the easy way. She had given into people like him for too long. And still she had suffered. Like there, out in the barn. No. This was the time when she was going to stop all that. Find some hidden strength, deep within, where she would show that she was not afraid. That he could not abuse her anymore. After all, the worse that could happen was that he could beat her to death. Strange, that did not seem to worry her now. After all, had she not experienced a type of living death, living as she had done under the same roof as her father and brother. Beaten or ridiculed nearly every day of her life. So did it really matter? At least this way, she may gain the satisfaction of letting him see that she was no longer afraid.

Leaving the half empty mug of tea on the hearth, she pulled the towel about her body and went up to her bedroom. Dog followed patiently behind, hoping for some form of recognition, but receiving none. His mistress was deep in thought; almost in a world of her own. She changed into a somber beige skirt, a plain top, a dark brown cardigan and a black pair of boots. Once she had combed and brushed her hair, bound it up beneath a black silk scarf she had found soon after her mother left, she studied herself in the full length mirror. Satisfied with her appearance, she returned to the parlour and unlocked the back door. Taking hold of the large length of beech wood resting near the door, she placed it on the floor near the hearth, turned her chair so it was facing the back door and gently lowered herself into it. Calling Dog to her side, she ordered him to lay still, and ignored his constant licking of her hand. She had much on her mind, and Dog did not understand.

Minutes ticked by from the old clock that stood on the mantle shelf above the fire and the sound appeared to calm her nerves. She was prepared to wait. She was in no hurry. There were none of the usual knots in her stomach. She was past all that now. No feeling of nausea, every time she heard a strange sound, wondering if it was Jacob returning. She was settled, relaxed. She had made up her mind, and destiny was about to take its course.

After some time the door to the back yard opened, and she looked up. Still there was no tension in her face. She was resigned to what she was about to do.

Expecting her elder brother, she was mildly surprised to see Giles enter, a smile on his face when he saw her, his school satchel slung over his shoulder.

"Jenny,' he said, with a broad beam across his face.

"You're home."

Crossing the room excitedly, he was surprised when she stopped him in his tracks.

"Shut the door," she said, with no emotion in her voice.

Whether it was the sound of her voice, or the look in her eyes, he could not be sure. But he knew he would be foolish to disobey. Once the door was shut, he crossed the room, slowly now, staring down at his sister, unable to understand what was wrong. He had not seen her for a week. Why was she not pleased to see him; as he was pleased to see her.

As he approached, he said "What happened to your face, Jen?" unable to miss the raw flesh and bruising around her cheeks, the black and purple marks down the sides of her neck. He would have seen more on her arms, had she not been wearing the long sleeved cardigan.

Staring at the back door, she seemed to ignore his question. She coughed once,. and winced at the pain in her ribs.

"Get to your room," she said quietly, but firmly.

"And stay there 'till you're called."

Giles was confused.

"But why, Jen? What's going on?" He asked.

Snapping her head sideways towards him, with venom in her eyes, she stared at him like she had never done before. And he was scared. Not just for him, but also for her. For her sanity. She looked so much like a woman he had seen one time in a black and white film, put on in the local village. A woman who, for some reason he could not remember, had turned mad. And done terrible things. And Jenny looked just like that woman now. That same look was in her eyes.

"Now!" she screeched like a banshee, a sound that would remain with him for the rest of his life. Scurrying up the stairs like a frightened rabbit, he darted into his bedroom and pulled the door almost shut. But he was curious too, and kept it just slightly ajar, so he would be able to listen to any sounds that came up from the parlour.

She turned back and settled into the chair, waiting for time to resume its patient course. Dog shifted a couple of times near the hearth, and sighed low and deep in his sleep. When the door opened again, he looked up and his body tensed.

Jenny's eyes studied her elder brother as he entered the room. His face was red and raw with fresh scratches on his face and down his arms. The earlier ones, down the left side of his face had opened up again. It looked a mess. His check shirt was hanging loose about the top of his trousers, and he swayed slightly as he entered the room. For a matter of seconds their eyes met, and for the first time ever, it was he who looked away first. It could have been guilt; it could have been fear. Who knows what? But he could see, even in the state he was, that his sister had changed. She was no more the little innocent girl. She almost reminded him of a she devil.

As he began to move forward, her eyes followed him. One step at a time. And he felt uneasy. Only once did he have the courage to stare at her. And when he looked away, that was when she spoke.

"And where do you think you're going?" she asked, in a voice that was full of menace and hatred that had bottled up over the years.

He turned to face her.

"What business is it of yours where I'm going?" he asked, feigning bravado.

She smiled. A broad smile that showed two rows of near perfect white teeth.. Almost a pleasant smile. But one that made him feel ill at ease. Not scared, but not far from it. Her eyes were like the eyes of a mad woman. Dark one minute, bright the next. Seeing all, yet not seeing. Aware, but not aware. A woman who, with little or no trouble, could stare deep into his own eyes and reach his very soul. He shivered and he wanted to leave. But he felt compelled to stay. It was like she was holding him in a trance. Under some sort of spell.

"I've made it my business, Jacob," she said in little more than a whisper.

"And you'll be doing exactly as I say."

Again her eyes stared deep into his, and he could not shake them. He felt compelled to look at her. Not to turn away.

"You see my face," she said, slowly and deliberately. And although he did not want to, he was nodding in agreement. She pointed slowly to the cuts, the abrasions and the bruises.

"You did that, Jacob" she said, in that quiet deliberate voice.

"You did that. And what's more, you defiled me."

He knew she was right. And he almost felt guilty. Looking at her now, dressed in those drab brown clothes, he could not imagine how he could have gone so far. To have forced himself upon her as he did. But then, seeing her in the barn, in that pure white cotton dress, clinging to her body where it was wet from the storm outside, he could not control himself. He knew he had been an animal. But that was the way he was. He had lost all control.

"And now," she said, in a firm but quiet voice, that he could barely hear, " You're going to leave."

He did not understand. She could tell that by the look on his face. And because he did not speak, she merely smiled.

"You're going to leave this farm now, Jacob. Never to return."

Still he was silent. What did she mean? True she appeared like a mad woman. But was she really mad. This was his farm. His birthright. Left to him by his father. And no scrawny slip of a girl was going to take it from him.

She was already reading his thoughts.

"Oh yes, Jacob" she smiled.

"You will be leaving. You can be sure of that. And shall I tell you why."

Still he remained silent, although he wanted to scream and shout some common sense into her. But he still felt compelled to listen.

And so she continued.

"You've got no alternative, Jacob. There is only one way you can go. Just look at my face. What you've done to me."

He looked at her, almost in a quizzical way, like he could not believe what he had done.

"And now," she said, turning to the mantel shelf above the fire, " look at yourself in the mirror, and tell me what you see."

Almost like he was doing her bidding, with Dog watching his every move from the comfort of the hearth, he crossed the room and, as she ordered him, so he studied his face in the mirror and was appalled at what he saw.

Turning to her, with anger in his eyes, he roared aloud.

"You did that to me, you whore. You did that."

Without flinching from the chair she smiled, and told Dog to sit up. Rising on his haunches, his eyes focused on Jacob, and he barely moved. But both man and beast knew who was master now.

"With a face like that," she said, cupping her hands in her lap, "folk would soon be asking questions of you. Especially as to what you got up to last night."

234

She paused, allowing the reality to sink in.

"As for my part, I'm quite ready to make a statement to the Police about what you did to me. So, if I'm thinking right, either way you'll be doing time inside."

Silence hung in the room for what seemed an eternity. Neither man, woman nor beast making a sound. And slowly, as time passed, as he remained calm, Jacob realised the finality of it all. Only once did he stare at Jenny again, with anger in his eyes. Her response was simple; and to the point. Turning her gaze to Dog she smiled, stroked his neck, and focused all her attention back to her brother.

"You'd be a fool to even think about it. I hate you, Jacob Couling. I curse the very ground you walk on. And if ever you tried to touch me again, I'll set him on you, let him rip you from limb to limb and leave you laying dead where you fall. Not a pretty sight. Just think on that Jacob. And now, make up your mind if you're about to leave."

DARK    SECRETS

PART    FOUR

ONE

Jenny needed time to think. Some time on her own. Jacob had left with a few
meager belongings, and now it was down to her to manage the farm. It would
not be easy, of that she was sure. But it never had been; and it probably never
would be.  Though at least now, with Jacob gone, she could live her life in
relative calm. Safe in the knowledge that she only had Giles and Dog to care
for.

She thought of Giles, alone upstairs, and called him down. He appeared white
and shaken, where he had heard some of the conversation, but not enough to
know what was really going on.

"Go and milk the cows for me," she said quietly, resting her hand on his arm.
"And see to the chickens."

She could not tell him the full story. Not yet, anyway. Although he was
desperate to know. She needed time to recover. To sort out her thoughts. She
promised she would tell him later, and smiled as he trotted off out through the
door. Still only a child, but old enough and strong enough to carry out a man's

work. And that's what he would have to do. Now, with his brother gone.

Jenny shivered. Probably the shock was coming out of her, and she grabbed her granny's shawl from behind the door. As she wrapped it around her shoulders, it gave her great comfort. She felt close, although she had been dead now for many a year. She wondered, as she passed through the door, closing it behind her, whether her granny would have been proud of her. And she believed she would.

Leaving Giles to carry out his chores, she turned right out of the garden gate and wandered off to the field known as three acre meadow. It was one of her favourite spots on the farm, especially the small copse, away on the far side. There she had spent many an hour, just sitting and thinking. And carrying out the odd drawing. With Dog lolloping by her side, she picked up the occasional twig and threw it absentmindedly, and Dog seemed most put out after he had taken the trouble to retrieve it, and she gave him no thanks. But Dog was the last thing on her mind at the moment. Although she realised she must keep him near her at all times, lest Jacob return. But there were far more pressing matters for her to resolve at the moment.

The number one priority was how she was going to run the farm. Jacob had never been a lot of good, but he did have muscle, and he had carried out jobs that required a man's strength when the fancy took him. But that was all over now. With just her and Giles to manage things, it would be a far different tale.

Luckily, he was just turned thirteen now, and could easily leave school, although she knew that wouldn't please him. He loved to learn, and he loved his school over at Buscot. Old Mr., Barnaby had nothing but praise for him, and often said that with a little more further education, he could go far. Unfortunately, that would not be the case now. Any ideas of further education were right out of the window. He was needed here, on the farm, and that was where he would have to stay. She dreaded the thought of telling him. It would certainly lead to a row. But she could cope with that. In a few days time. When she was a little stronger. When things had settled down.

Then there was the actual running of the farm. Organising the day to day routine. Planning ahead over the next few months. There would be a lot to do and a lot to think about. And she had to admit that the thought of it excited her more than a little. Never before had she been allowed to make decisions. Only told what to do. And if she refused, which was very rare, or messed things up, then she received a good hiding for her troubles. But not any more. Now she was mistress of Holly Bank Farm. Whether by choice or design. And it was down to her whether it succeeded or failed. With a smile on her face, she grabbed Dog tightly around the neck and threw him gently to the ground, so he rolled away from her, kicking his legs in the air as he tried to free himself from her grasp, before leaping up and careering off across the field. She smiled and chuckled as she watched him run, and as she followed, she wondered just what type of farmer she would be.

# TWO

That night, after all the chores were done, the cows milked, the pigs fed and the chicken locked up for the night, she sat Giles down and told him what had happened out there in the barn that afternoon. Well, not all. That would have been too much for both of them to bear. But enough. Just enough for him to know why their brother could not remain. Why he had decided to leave. Unfortunately, Giles would never know the whole truth. Not as it really happened. And she thought that was a shame. He was entitled to know. It was his right. But she could not tell him. And she prayed to God he would never find out.

As the days passed, she got word to Chas that she needed his help. Three store cattle had been culled from her small beef herd, destined for the market at Fairford, and true to his word, he arrived with his cattle lorry at nine thirty on the Friday morning. Giles was the first to greet him. Struggling with a pitch fork load of straw as he crossed the yard to the milk shed, he was pleased for a rest and lowered the fork to the ground.

"You not at school today," asked Chas, climbing down from his lorry, having parked it near the gate that led into the garden alongside the house.

Giles shook his head.

"Too much to do here," he said.

"Now that Jacob's gone."

Jenny was surprised how well he had taken the news that he would be leaving school and help her out on the farm. She had expected at worst a blazing row. At best a week long sulk. Fortunately, he had taken the news well, and now they were alone, he had buckled down and was doing more than his fair share of work around the farm. Without Jacob badgering him, it was like he had taken on a new purpose in life. As if he was trying to show her he was in fact, a young man.

"I had heard," replied Chas, leaning against the cab.

"What happened?"

Giles heaved the fork back onto his shoulder and nodded towards the house, not wanting to get into any conversation that involved Jacob.

"You'd best ask Jenny about that. She's waiting for you inside."

With that he was gone, striding off across the yard, leaving Chas to ponder on. As he watched, the family friend noticed a slight change in the young boy. As though he had not only grown in stature, but in maturity as well, and was already taking on the place of his elder brother who had left them in the lurch. Walking towards the back door, he wondered what it was all about, and whether some of the tales he had heard round about were true. Maybe only time would tell.

Jenny greeted him with a smile and invited him in, offering him a mug of tea as she closed the door behind them.

"It was good of you to come, "she said, as he took a chair and watched her pour tea from the pot into a couple of mugs.

"You got the message all right then."

He nodded. It was amazing how, in those days, messages could be passed around the countryside from one person to another, without the need for telephones or other modern day equipment. Just a mention from Jenny, to Sam the local postman, that she had need of Chas's lorry for Friday morning, and by the end of the day it was all arranged.

As he watched her he could see the marks and bruises about her face, although she had done well to cover those around her neck with a scarf.

"Is that what he did to you?" he asked, as she slowly crossed the room and placed the two mugs down on the table.

"Who?" she asked, lowering herself into a chair so she was facing him, but her eyes not looking at him.

"You know who," he replied, sounding more than a little annoyed.

"Your brother. Jacob. That's who"

They stared across the table at each other. Two friends, who rarely saw each other. But he was always there when she needed him. She was the first to lower her gaze.

"I'd rather not talk about him," she said, tasting the sweetness of the tea and enjoying it.

"He's gone, and that's an end to it."

"I'll be damned if it is," snapped Chas, screwing up his flat cap so tightly that she realised just how much power he had in those hands.

"He's done something pretty awful to you, of that I'm sure. And I reckon I have as much right as anyone to know what it is. More in fact, if the truth be known."

That last sentence took her by surprise.

"And why's that, Chas?" she asked, looking at him calmly, wondering why he thought he was more entitled than anyone else to know her darkest secrets.

He realised he'd said more than he should have done, and was already feeling a little awkward. In fact, he was beginning to blush. For a moment he looked away, around the room. Anywhere so he didn't have to look at her. But then he took a deep breath, turned back towards the table and tried again to say his piece.

"Because I like you," he blurted out, in such a way that he realised it sounded stupid. Like the ramblings of an idiot. No sooner had he said those four simple words, than he began to wish he hadn't.

Jenny smiled, leant forward and would have placed her hand on his arm, to thank him and reassure him. But she was not ready for that. There was no way she could ever touch another man. Not after what Jacob had done to her. But she still liked Chas as a true friend, and had done so for some time. And she told him so.

It was not quite the response he was hoping for. Somewhere deep down, he was wishing that she may have felt the same way for him as he did for her. That she really cared for him. But from her last remark, that didn't seem very likely, and maybe it was best to say no more on the subject.

They remained silent for a while. Both staring into their cups, each with there own thoughts. And they both felt comfortable. Yet normally, when two people are together, unless they have that special bond where they are almost two people as one, there can be a sense of unease. Awkwardness even. Yet there was none of this with Chas and Jenny. They were just quiet, and appeared to be contented.

Eventually it was Chas who spoke.

"I'd best get these store cattle loaded then," he said, looking up into her eyes, taking his cap in his hand.

"That is if you're not going to tell me what happened."

She smiled back at him.

"There's nothing to tell. Nothing much happened. It was mainly my fault anyway."

He stood up and placed the cap on his head.

"Of course it was," he said bluntly and walked towards the back door. As he reached the far side of the room he turned.

"Just remember," he said, with no expression on his face.

"If I ever see him again, I'll kill him. I won't be able to stop myself."

Then he was gone.

And Jenny was left to ponder on what had been said.

## THREE

True to his word, Chas took the three store cattle to market and entered them in Jenny's name. They fetched a fair price, and he returned with her cash the following day. It was not a fortune, but it would tide her over the next few weeks. Along with the milk money from the local creamery every day, a few dozen eggs sold to the village shop, and ten pork pigs due to be slaughtered in a few weeks time, she could get by. But she knew, with winter only a few months away, she would need to earn some extra cash.

Drawing seemed to be the answer, and over the next few weeks, she managed to draw a number of sketches, both of wild life and birds, and one or two excellent scenes of early morning mist rising over the fields. Dog was her model on two or three sketches, but even she had to admit that there was little likelihood that they would ever sell. Poor old Dog, he was far too ugly. But she felt the others were passable.

She wrote to Peter Laughton that she had more works available, and he replied by return of post that he was more than interested in viewing them. Thankfully, the marks on her face had now healed. The only remaining sign to Jacob's brutality was the fading of a bruise on the left side of her neck. A long, dark blue mark that could have been caused by his thumb. She covered this with a blue silk scarf that she felt comfortable with, and wore a plain white cotton skirt with a colorful floral top. She topped all this with her Granny's shawl, for it was a windy day, and hoped the shawl may bring her luck. When she told Chas of her forthcoming visit to the gallery in Cheltenham, he was more than happy to offer her a lift in his lorry, and she was more than happy to accept. She was glad she was with him on the drive over there. He was probably one of her closest friends, and they were good company together.

He kept saying how proud he was to know an artist who was about to become famous, and although she smiled and thanked him on the first occasion, by the seventh or eighth, the flattery was wearing a little thin. But for all that, his conversation was interesting most of the way to Cheltenham, and it calmed her nerves. They chatted about all manner of things, from the weather, the up and coming harvest festival to be held at the Nags Head in two weeks time, and even old Mrs. Beaton, who had to be in her late forties, and just given birth to a set of triplets. Something almost unheard of in those parts.

Chas offered to carry her portfolio into the gallery, but she declined, and suggested he call back within half an hour, if that was all right with him. Once he had helped her down from the cab, he agreed to call back once he had carried out some business with a local farmer, not a mile or two out of town, and would meet up with her later.

Watching her struggling in the wind as she carried the drawings up the steps towards the gallery entrance, he wished she had accepted his offer to help, but our Jenny, he thought, was becoming a little bit more independent of late, and he wasn't too sure that he liked the change in her. But then he thought, as his Mum always says, everything and everybody must change as time goes on. That's what life is all about. And so it was. With a toot on the horn and a wave of his hand, he shrugged his shoulders and smiled. Jenny turned to wave him off, and soon he was trundling off down the road, heading out of Cheltenham, hoping to earn a few extra bob from a business acquaintance. After all, winter was coming on, and he knew times would be hard again for fellers the like of him.

Jenny entered "Laughton's Fine Art Gallery "at twelve thirty p.m. with a sense of apprehension which was not unnatural for a shy quiet country girl like her. Wide frontal windows allowed passers by to stare in at her, as she stood waiting to be approached, and the large white painted walls appeared cold and clinical. The floor was constructed of modern day pine, which clunked and clanked with every footstep she took. The majority of the paintings on show, lined up in military fashion down the center of each wall, were not, in the main, to her liking. She preferred the more traditional style, as it was called. Paintings of birds, animals and scenery that looked like birds, animals and scenery. What they were meant to look like. Not some odd colours slapped together that formed circles or squares; or trickles of paint allowed to run all over the canvas in any way they wished. That was not real painting. Not according to Jenny.

A young woman in a brown two piece suit, with an hour glass figure, approached from the far end of the gallery. Only three other people were present. A couple in their early twenties, who wanted the whole world and his wife to know they were exponents of fine art. And an elderly gent, sitting on a bench, who had obviously come in out of the cold, and intended to stay as long as he could, before he was told to leave. He was staring vacantly at a canvas, portraying a mixture of blue, yellow and red daubs of paint, that were supposed to represent something, but he wasn't sure what.

"May I help you," asked the young woman approaching Jenny, with an air of haughtiness about her. The thick rimmed glasses made her appear even more severe than she probably was, but this did not make Jenny feel any the less apprehensive as she approached.

Jenny explained her reason for visiting the gallery.

"Ah yes," replied the woman, looking down at her, for she was considerably taller than Jenny.

"Mr. Laughton did mention you were coming."

She paused, studying this girl, who appeared more of a waif than a potential artist.

"Unfortunately, he has been called away on urgent business. But he did instruct me to view your paintings on his behalf and give you some advice."

Jenny felt somewhat put out as she followed the woman down the gallery to a small office set off to the side, but she said nothing. After making the effort to come all this way from Buscot, the very least she expected was for Peter Laughton to be here to greet her. Not some bespectacled woman who obviously thought she was far more superior than she actually was.

"By the way, I'm Miss Prentice" said the other woman, offering Jenny a chair, whilst she remained standing.

"I expect Mr., Laughton told you about me."

Jenny shook her head and said "No, I don't think so," as she made rather a hash of pulling the drawings from her portfolio. Not a thing she was used to doing.

Miss Prentice looked somewhat surprised.

"Are you sure?" she asked, taking hold of one of the drawings and studying it at some length.

With the last drawing free, Jenny sat upright in the chair and said "I think I'd have remembered if he had."

Miss Prentice studied each drawing in turn, and each one in detail.

"Is this all you have?" she asked, rather disappointed.

Jenny said it was, and she had already told Peter how many to expect.

"I don't think there are enough here for an exhibition," smiled Miss Prentice, rather wryly.

"I wasn't expecting an Exhibition," said Jenny.

"If they were good enough, then I expected them to be hung along with my others in the gallery. If there was room."

From her chair, Jenny had to turn to look out at the gallery, and noticed three of her drawings hanging off to the right, along with one of her Mothers. Two of hers depicted swans on the lake, up near the copse in three acre meadow, and one of a fox she had spotted early one morning, on its return home to its lair, following a night of hunting.

"Have any more of mine sold?" asked Jenny eagerly, as Miss Prentice continued studying the drawing of a heron on a branch, watching a fish in the water. She had to admit to herself it was very good.

"Two recently," she said with an air of indifference, placing the drawing back on the pile, along with the others.

"And there has been interest in one of Amanda Beckworth's. I believe she's related to you," she said casually, lowering herself into the chair opposite Jenny, and reaching down for a cheque book from one of the drawers in the desk.

Jenny turned abruptly and faced her.

"One of Mum's," she gasped, full of surprise.

Miss Prentice nodded, but did not enlighten her any more. She was busy filling in a cheque made out to Jenny Couling.

"Which one?" Asked Jenny, leaning forward in her chair, full of curiosity.

Miss Prentice remained silent until she had completed the cheque. Then, shaking it gently in the air to encourage the ink to dry she said "The portrait of a young girl."

As she handed the completed cheque to Jenny, explaining that she had Peter Laughton's authority to write cheques in his absence, she added, almost as an afterthought, "In fact, the model looks a lot like you."

Jenny took the cheque, but seemed to ignore its contents. Cupping her hands to her mouth she gasped.

"It was me," she replied. "When I was a child."

Miss Prentice, now filling out a receipt, gave a half hearted smile and said "Your Mother is a very talented artist. I can see where your talent comes from."

Jenny was not used to such compliments, and had never expected them to come from the likes of Miss Prentice. Still with cheque in hand, she remained silent as Miss Prentice completed a receipt for the new drawings, and, after the customary shake in the air, handed it to Jenny.

"What's this for," she asked, unaware, as yet, of the necessities of such forms when conducting business.

Miss Prentice explained, with a deep sigh, and asked Jenny to sign a well worn ledger that showed she had received her cheque to the amount of five guineas, less commission. Jenny, unaware until now of the size of the cheque, appeared most surprised.

"Is anything wrong?" asked Miss Prentice, wondering if she had made some error in the ledger.

"Oh no," replied Jenny.

"Nothing's wrong. I just wasn't expecting this much, that's all."

Miss Prentice smiled and guided Jenny's hand to the point in the ledger where her signature was required.

"An artist who can produce your quality of work must expect sums such as these, and hopefully more as you become well known."

Jenny felt very proud, and would have enjoyed the compliment, if only she had known how to sign her signature. Unfortunately, there had never been any reason for her to sign for anything in the past, what with her father and Jacob carrying out all business transactions on the farm. Although she had heard of people making their mark with an 'x', she hardly felt that course of action was appropriate now. Fortunately Miss Prentice sensed her dilemma, and surprisingly, offered to help her solve the problem.

"I assume you have no suitable signature as yet. Not one that would be acceptable for your artistic work."

It was more of a statement than a question, but Jenny shook her head anyway.

"A situation common with many an artist," lied Miss Prentice, who seemed to have warmed towards this young girl who herself showed a great deal of warmth and compassion. She knew she felt ill at ease, and did not wish to cause her any further embarrassment.

"May I?" she asked, taking the pen from Jenny's hand, and with a few deft strokes, had supplied three possibilities from which Jenny could choose. Jenny smiled and thanked her, and copied the one that looked easiest. After all, writing had never been her strong point. Miss Prentice handed her the shred of paper with the three signatures and said "You'd better keep this. It takes a while to find a signature that really suites you. It may well be that you decide on one entirely of your own choice."

The two women smiled and a bond had been formed.

Miss Prentice guided her from the office to the exit door and said "Only time will tell."

# FOUR

As days turned into weeks Jenny grew stronger. With the help of Giles and the occasional visit from Chas, the farm was slowly taking shape. She now had a plan. The milking herd was slowly building, where she had recently bought in a couple of freshly calved heifers. Three more store cattle had been sent to market, along with the litter of black and white piglets born sixteen weeks earlier, and the Rhode Island red hens were laying well since a new cockerel had been brought in to spice them up a bit. Jenny had even taken up Chas's offer to join him at the Harvest Home Supper at the Nag's Head, after a great deal of cajoling. Although she only accompanied him in a couple of dances on the floor, and turned down all offers from other young country lads, she had to admit she enjoyed the evening. She also surprised herself when, as they arrived home at Holly Bank Farm, she did not withdraw when Chas planted a gentle kiss on her forehead before bidding her good night. But that was all. No fondling, or cuddling. And she was glad he had not tried to coax her. She was not ready for that sort of thing, and in all probability, would not be for a long time to come.

One morning, not long after the Harvest Home Supper, whilst she was supping tea during her mid morning break, Jenny received a visitor from the Lechlade Constabulary. Sergeant Dicks had known the Couling family for many years, and back a while; he would not have received a cordial greeting. But Jenny invited him in, offered him a chair at the table, and poured a sweet mug of tea along with a good slice of home made bread topped with a wedge of butter that melted down the sides, where the bread was still warm. As she joined him, Sergeant Dicks explained the purpose of his visit.

"It seems that brother of yours has been up to no good," he said, taking a great bite of bread and forcing Jenny to wait until he had finished chewing before he was in a position to enlighten her. It could have been either brother he was referring to, but in her heart Jenny knew it was Jacob.

"What is it?" she asked flatly, trying to speed him up a bit.

Finally he continued.

It seemed Jacob had been living rough since leaving Holly Bank Farm. Ducking here, diving there. A little bit of thieving in one place, a burglary in another. Anything to keep body and soul together. And whilst the local Police knew what he had been up to, and they had pulled him in a few times for questioning, he would never give them the time of day, and they could never prove anything against him.

"So why have you come to see me?" asked Jenny, more than a little concerned.

Sergeant Dicks took another mouthful of the delicious sweet tea and leant back in the chair with his arms folded over a protruding belly. At any other time he would have been a jocular fellow. But this was serious business, and he kept his composure.

"The truth is, Jenny" he said, slowly and deliberately, "your brother Jacob has got himself into a bit more serious trouble this time. It seems that for the past month or so he's been hanging around out Witney way. Don't ask me why, because I don't know. But at least it kept him out of our hair. Anyhow, last night he takes a notion into his head that he's going to do a burglary, which he does, and it all goes wrong. He beats someone up pretty bad and steals a shot gun. Luckily he didn't get any cartridges with it; because the owner had them hidden away separate, like. But the Witney lads think he might be heading this way where it's too hot for him up there now."

Jenny trembled slightly, and it did not go unnoticed by the Sergeant. She shared a secret with Jacob that no one else knew. And if he was coming back this way, then she had great cause to be frightened.

"What is it, lass?" asked the Sergeant in a sympathetic voice, as he lowered his mug to the table.

She shook her head and said "Nothing."

Sergeant Dicks gave a friendly smile that Jenny had not been accustomed to. It was somewhere between the smile of a father and the smile of a friend. And she almost felt that she could trust him.

"You don't have to tell me anything, of course," he said, leaning forward in his chair, so he was that much closer to her.

"But you've seen him recently, haven't you."

It wasn't a question; more a statement of fact. Jenny shook her head, but did not speak.

"It's all right, lass," he said quietly, and with a good long pause. "You don't have to say anything you don't want to. Not right now. But at times like this it can help to talk it over with a friend."

He was a wily old fox, was Sergeant Dicks. He had a way with words, and a countenance to match. And he could usually unravel a mystery, whether it be from a hardened criminal, or a poor simple country girl like Jenny. It was just a matter of time and perseverance. And so it was, as the clock over the fire place ticked on, and Dog gave the occasional grunt as he stirred in his sleep, the truth began to emerge.

Not six weeks back, Jenny had been out in the yard tending the animals, when she heard a noise coming from one of the barns. Calling Dog to her side, she went to investigate, only to find her brother Jacob hiding inside. She had to admit that he was a far different sight than when she last saw him. Covered in grime and dirt, and weighing at least half what he used to before he left, his beard was matted and his hair was a tangled mass. And he still frightened her. But Dog stood close by, with bristles up along his back, and a snarl across his mouth. Jenny gave Jacob the time of day to explain the purpose of his visit, and although she would never allow him back on the farm and keep silent about what had occurred, which he pleaded her to consider, she still felt sorry for him and gave him some fresh clothes that belonged to their father, along with a couple of loaves of bread, some cheese and a cut of freshly cured ham. And then she sent him on his way. But not before he vowed he would return some day and take back what was rightfully his. And she would rue the day she decided that she would cross him. With tears in her eyes she began to tremble and clasped her small white hands tightly together in her lap.

"There, there now, don't fret, lass." said the Sergeant with a quiet calm voice. "We'll see no harm comes to you, don't you worry about that."

Grand words indeed, and very comforting too. But not always that easy to carry out. But his intentions were good. And as they chatted, so it all came out. Soon Sergeant Dicks knew all he needed to know about what had gone on at Holly Bank Farm over a good number of years. And he felt sorry for the poor young girl now sitting opposite him.

But such feelings could not be dwelt upon. There were things to be done. And although his countenance tended to point to the contrary, Sergeant Dicks was actually a man of action, when the need arose.

Within the hour a team of uniformed officers from surrounding stations, with shovels and pick axes to hand, had peeled off their tunics and were pulling up the earthen floor of the barn to the left of the cowshed. A couple of Alsatian dogs sniffed here and there, as they ran to and fro with their handlers, and one found great pleasure in cocking his leg at a hawthorn bush every time he passed. Even the local Detective Sergeant had arrived on the scene, along with his sidekick, a scruffy looking individual, who belched quite frequently, and the two of them spent most of the afternoon leaning against the five bar wooden gate that marked the entrance to the farm, waiting for news of some heinous crime, but neither really expecting anything to come of it.

But, as is so often the case, when one does not expect something interesting to happen, it so very often does. And such was the case now, on a cool late afternoon towards the end of Autumn, down at Holly Bank Farm, set in the peaceful meandering landscape of Gloucestershire.

"Over here, Serge," shouted one of the constables in the customary manner that is so often seen on films, but rarely happens in true life.

"I think I've found something."

And of course he had. For no self respecting officer of the law would intimate that he had found something important appertaining to a possible crime, unless he was pretty damn sure himself before hand that he had. So when Sergeant Dicks and the two Cid officers hurried into the barn and scrambled over a great heap of dirt that had been piled up high, there was every chance they would see the remains of a corpse staring back up at them from down below in the hole that had been excavated.

Now he had a possible crime to work on the Detective Sergeant took control and put plans into motion, leaving Sergeant Dicks to handle the more mundane matters, as was common in circumstances of this nature. First and foremost he had to cover his back. With the assistance of a uniformed officer on a bicycle, word was sent to the next officer in the chain of command; a Detective Inspector who was now sitting in a comfortable office over at Cirencester. The local doctor was called to certify death, although that was hardly necessary from the state of the body, and the scenes of crimes boys were soon aware that they would be working overtime tonight.

Jenny looked up from the table, where she had been talking to Giles, as Sergeant Dicks knocked the door and walked in. Treating the parlour as his own, he found a vacant chair and joined the two youngsters, before removing his helmet and placing it on the table before him. He explained what had been found so far and Jenny turned white. Gile's mouth dropped, but he said nothing.

"It's a sorry business," he sighed, looking at Jenny.

"But 'twas best you told us when you did."

Jenny nodded, but did not feel any easier by his remarks.

"Have you any idea who it is?" she asked, shivering slightly.

The Sergeant shook his head and said not yet, but they would find out soon enough, and suggested she make a brew to take her mind off things.

. The County pathologist suggested that, from his examination in situ, the victim, which was a female, had been strangled. It was far too early to give any more detail at this stage, and the Police would have to wait until the following day for a more detailed examination.

None of this comforted Jenny, and she was mightily relieved when Sergeant Dicks, later that evening, as he prepared to leave, informed her that a uniformed officer would be standing guard over the gruesome find for the rest of the night, and another would be outside the house for her protection. If she was worried or had any cause for concern, then she should not hesitate to give one of them a shout. She smiled, thanked him for his help, and said that she would. Closing the door behind him, she turned, leant against it heavily, and let out a deep sigh, realising for the first time that day how utterly exhausted she was. Looking down at Dog she whispered " I think its time we went to bed, don't you."

Dog stared up at her and wagged his tail, as if he knew exactly what she was talking about, although he probably had no idea at all. Leaving him to guard the parlour, she slowly climbed the stairs, and with the sound of Giles deep breathing coming from his bedroom, she knew he was already asleep.

# FIVE

The night duty policeman stared down at the deep hole in the ground and shivered. Whether it was the thought of a lost soul being taken from this earth, or the chill of the night air, he could not be sure, but it was enough to make him draw the heavy serge cape tighter around his shoulders and stamp his feet. Pulling a base metal watch from his inside pocket, he could see from a shaft of moonlight, shining through a gap in the wall, that it was fast approaching three o'clock. Like every other policeman, he hated the coming hour. If you failed to fall asleep at some time between the hour of three and four o'clock in the morning, you could be considered a hero. It was almost impossible to stay awake. Already he was yawning, and the eyes felt heavy. They ached and he gave them a good hard rub. Taking the lamp from its hook on the wall, he checked the reservoir for oil, trimmed the wick, and ventured outside. Anything to break this damned monotonous boredom. The moon, bright and silver, was high in the sky, but had already started its downward track towards the Western horizon. A few more hours and it would disappear from sight, only to be replaced by a new sun, rising again over to the East.

Strange, he thought, how life goes on. One day leading into the next. One life being taken today, only to be replaced by another; or maybe two or three or four. Time never stood still. It was not in its nature. And how ever hard you tried to figure it out, you could bet you never could.

Hearing the snap of a twig, he backed into a limited amount of shadow offered by one of the barns. With the moon so high, the shadows fell short, but it was enough. Hiding the lamp behind his back he stood and listened. There it was again. Only closer this time. Or so it seemed. As he waited, he listened for other sounds. And there were many. Especially for this time of night. A bird, startled by an animal, somewhere in the distance, flapped its wings and screeched a warning. A dog fox, way off across the hills, made its eerie banshee sound that sent shivers running down his spine. How he hated that sound. For all the time he had lived in the country, he had never grown accustomed to it.

But it did not bother Jacob. He had grown used to the sounds of the night. Ever since he had been turned away from Holly Bank Farm. But he was back now, ready to seek his revenge. But as he watched the copper, from the security of the stable door opposite, he wondered why he was here. At this time, just when he wanted no witnesses.

He too was feeling the chill of the night, and pulled the trench coat he had stolen from a disabled tramp, up around his shoulders. Like the copper opposite, he had heard the twigs break, but being a country lad, he guessed it was a badger, out for its nightly search of worms. And he wasn't far wrong. Except there were two of them. And they grunted to each other as they passed.

The Policeman smiled as he watched them, and rolled himself a cigarette.

Lighting it from the oil lamp, he inhaled deeply and the cold air, mixed with smoke, hitting the very depths of his lungs, made him feel good. He watched the exhaled smoke drift slowly away on the cold night air, and as it curled and twisted, he cursed to himself. Had he not promised his wife, just a few hours earlier, that he would give up? If not for his sake, then at least for the sake of the children. Of course, he could not see it was harmful. In those days, around 1928, no one much thought that tobacco smoke didn't do you a lot of good. But his pretty young wife was probably born before her time, and because he loved her, he threw it to the ground and crushed it beneath his boot.

Jacob watched and waited patiently. He wasn't bothered. He had all night. All he had to do was bide his time. Wait until the copper was out of the way and then he could make his way to the farm house and carry out the awful deed. He would make sure that his sister suffered for all the heart ache she had caused.

As he watched the copper turn and walk back into the barn, he wondered why he was here. It didn't make sense. Unless it was because they were after him. But that wouldn't make sense either. Not this soon after the burglary and the hijacking. After all, coppers weren't that bright. Not round this way, anyhow.

Moving to a more comfortable position behind the stable door, he felt the shotgun, tied up with a length of string, around his shoulder, and it felt good. Thinking of how he came by it made him smile. Initially it had all been so simple. A straight forward burglary in a well to do detached house just outside of Witney town. There would be cash and food there. Just what he needed to last a few more days, before he could find somewhere else to rob. Gaining entry had been a piece of cake. An old worn sash window to the side of the rear door gave way without too much pressure. It was small, but still large enough to take his arm, and soon he was turning the key in the lock. Once inside and it didn't take too many brains to figure out where the parlour was, and after he'd loaded the hessian sack he carried with a few victuals and a bottle of claret, he was off into the room that housed the silver. But that was where it all went wrong. Unbeknown to Jacob, although it was well past two thirty in the morning, the master was still up and reading in the library. Hearing movement in the room next door, he took down the heavily engraved shot gun from its resting place on the wall, and was about to unlock the box that contained the cartridges, when Jacob tripped and fell over a plant stand near the large bay window in the drawing room. Such a commotion caused the owner of the property to forget about the cartridges, and with his mind set on only one thing, thundered through the door into the next room, only to meet Jacob, face to face. For a matter of seconds, both men stared at each other in the silver light given off by a distant moon. The master of the house was well turned out in a fine Worsted three piece suit. Jacob on the other hand, was little more than a tramp, with matted hair that had grown long over the past weeks, a grubby beard, and dirt caked trousers and jacket to match. He was the first to move. Although both barrels were pointed directly at him, he took the initiative and swung his arm up in a wide arc, catching the other man off balance, sending both man and shotgun to the floor with an almighty rattle. Expecting a roar from both barrels, Jacob froze momentarily, but when none came, he bent forward to seize the gun. The owner of the property reached up in a half hearted attempt to stop his assailant, but Jacob was ready for him, and with both boots, waded into the poor unfortunate man until he resembled little more than pulped flesh.

Laughing like someone possessed, he gathered up the shotgun and was away. With his trench coat flapping out behind, he was running off out of the building and down the driveway into an empty street. There he disappeared once more into the darkness and was lost from sight.

If he had remained out of sight for the remainder of the night, then all may have been well. At least for a few days. But the feel of the shotgun in his hands gave him a sense of power, and already he was beginning to feel invincible. So much so that he loaded the gun with cartridges he had stolen from a previous burglary, because they were there available, and he thought they may come in useful, and hijacked a car in the early hours of the morning, ordering the terrified driver to drive him to Fairford. Once there, he roped and gagged the poor unfortunate and bundled him into the boot of the car, not caring whether he lived or died, and disappeared into the countryside, where he was to spend the remainder of the day. Fortunately the car was left near the town center, where unbeknown to Jacob, a passer by heard knocking sounds coming from inside and alerted the Police. The driver, when recovered from his ordeal, was able to give a concise account of his attacker, and the description was passed to all neighbouring stations.

Jacob, meanwhile, had remained undetected for the whole day, as he wandered the fields and the hedgerows, waiting for night fall to come. Somewhere around midnight  he found a car that suited his purpose, and after tweaking the ignition wires with the skill of an expert, he drove towards Lechlade and out onto the Buscot road, stopping well short of Holly Bank Farm by some half a mile, and dousing the lights and engine. From here on in it was easy. He could read the lie of the land like the back of his hand, and in no time at all was resting in the stable, waiting for the right moment to come. That was the very time though, when he became aware of the copper, who put him on his guard.

His head was still spinning in circles as he tried to figure out why the copper was here. It irked him ragged. And why in the barn. That particular barn. The one to the left of the cowshed. Then slowly, very slowly, it began to dawn on him. Of course. That was where the body lay. The tart, who had scratched his face so badly, leaving four great weal's running down the side of his cheek that had taken weeks to heal. That was it. But how could the law have found out. The tart was no more than a traveling girl; just passing through the area with her family. A tart who wanted a one night stand and then changed her mind. No one would miss her. Besides, he knew the family had left the district within a few days, so they would never be able to trace where she was. So how had the coppers found out? There had to be someone who told them. Spilled the beans and dropped him right in it. And the more he thought, the more he began to realise. Of course. it could be only one person. There had to be just one person. Jenny. She had done it again. Opened her mouth to someone and blabbered all about it. Told them how she had seen the weal's on his face and was unsure how they got there. How she had seen him coming from the barn on the afternoon of the thunderstorm. How he had caught her near the makeshift grave and had his way with her. Even now, the very thought of her excited his distorted mind. But anger was stronger than lust at this moment in time, and he thought more on the future than the past.

Dear sweet Jenny; the girl everyone thought was so wonderful, so perfect. And now she was about to suffer, like she had never suffered before.

Hoisting the shotgun high on his shoulder, he eased himself through the stable door, and made his way silently towards the farm house, ever watchful of the old barn door, lest the copper inside reappear. Another dog fox shrieked its eerie bark on the cool night air, away in the distance, almost as a warning for the evil that was about to befall Holly Bank Farm that night.

# SIX

Jenny tossed and turned in her bed as strange thoughts, mixed with dreams, swirled around through the passages of her tormented mind. Pictures of her mother's face, no longer the beauty she had once been, but a twisted and distorted hag, with long grey matted hair, smiled down upon her, swaying slowly back and forth, before disappearing into a shroud of mist, only to be replaced by the face of her father, unshaven and grinning, with eyes so evil she could feel herself grow taught with fear, even though she was half asleep. One moment laughing, the next snarling; but forever the controller of her small and precious world. And then he too was gone into the mists, only to return at a later time. Dog came to her that night. Not as an old and friendly companion as he had always been. But a vicious, snapping, growling beast, with stinking breath and deep red eyes. Stained brown teeth, forever coming closer and closer, snapping at her hands, her face, her body. For ever to gain revenge. But why. What had she ever done to upset them? She had always tried to be a good and honest person. She could not understand. Yet they were here. One after the other. And then there were more. Faces she had seen over the years. Some she knew well; others she recalled, from way back in the distant past. But barely knew them. Merely acquaintances. But they were all there. They had all come to see her. To peer down upon her and vent their wrath. Everything, they seemed to say, that she had done in her life, was to cause them harm and anguish. To each and every one of them. And now she must suffer the consequences. For this was the night she must surely pay.

A mighty blast suddenly ripped through the night. The sound shattered the images running through her mind into a thousand pieces and she sat bolt upright in her bed. The moon was bright that night and shone through her bedroom window, lighting up the room in a dull blue silver tone. She was shaking and was not sure whether it was the reaction from her dreams or the sound of the blast. Desperately she tried to clear her mind, to work out what had caused the sound. It came so suddenly, without warning that she could not grasp the situation. It was the same reaction most people experience when woken from a deep sleep with a sudden shock. That part of the mind that should tell you where you are will not respond. You stare vacantly all around like some zombie, eyes wide but seeing nothing. As if you are in another world. And such was the case with Jenny. Turning her head this way and that, she blinked, breathed quietly and listened. Instinctively she knew it spelt trouble. But from whom, and for whom.

Although she thought an age had passed, it was no more than seconds, and she could hear a man screaming; and then Dog barking loudly down in the parlour. The sound coming from the man was short, sharp, intermittent shrieks, followed by just the odd dull groan. The sound seemed to be coming from under her open window, and still in a daze she wondered somewhat foolishly, if it was the policeman, then how could he protect her. Gathering a sheet around her body, she climbed from her bed, and was half way across the room when the door flew open. Giles, with face as white as the sheet she had wrapped around her shoulders, stared at Jenny and whispered "What was that?"

Jenny raised her finger to her lips, bidding him be quiet, and pointed to the window. Creeping across the bare pine floor boards, she beckoned that he follow, and as they reached their destination, she ordered him to kneel down below the window sill. Already she could hear the man moaning down below, and cautiously raised her head for a clearer view. Her eyes were now accustomed to the light, for it was brighter outside than in the room, and peering down, she could see a crumpled body laying bent double amongst the shrubs that bordered the gravel path leading around the side of the building. Whether he was dead or badly injured, she could not tell, for he was no longer making any sound, but away across the yard she could see another policeman running from the barn. With lamp held high, the flame flickering in the night, he gave Jacob the opportunity of a perfect shot and Jenny could see her brother raising the shot gun to his shoulder and taking aim.

"No! No!" she screamed, leaning out of the window, having scant regard for her own safety.

"Go back! He's going to shoot!"

Giles, ignoring his sister's earlier warning, rose from the floor, and he too leaned from the window, eager to see what was going on. The two of them watched as the policeman, a tall lean man somewhere in his thirties, continued to run towards the house. . But now he had thrown the oil lamp to one side, unaware of the small blast as it bounced off the barn wall and spluttered into flames, and was zig zagging to one side and then the other as he desperately tried to foil Jacob's attempts to aim.

"Where is he?" he screamed to the two youngsters as he darted towards the low stone wall that separated the yard from the garden.

"Is he left or right of the gate?"

Giles was about to shout "Left", but Jenny was now wide awake and realised just in time how easy it was to make a mistake.

"To your right!" she screamed, hoping he could hear her.

"He's to your right!"

Giles looked back at Jenny, about to correct her, then, as his jaw dropped, realised the awful truth. What if he had shouted out the first thought that came to his mind. Turning back to the scene outside, with head craned forward, he could just make out the silhouette of the policeman leap the gate with his cape flowing out behind. Whilst still in mid air he was turning to his right and Giles and Jenny could see Jacob kneeling amongst the shrubs bringing the shotgun to bear on his adversary. The end was quick, and probably quite painless. The

273

single blast echoed around the farm and the policeman was dead before he hit the ground. Jacob, now covered in the other man's blood, pushed him to one side and turned to look up at his siblings, staring down from the window.

"Thought you would save him, aye?" he laughed, with such glee that he sounded like he was turning mad.

"Well, it looks like it's going to be your turn next."

After placing two more cartridges into the breach, he rose with the shot gun to his full height and turned once more on the youngsters, unaware that the old barn next to the cowshed was turning into a glowing blaze of crackling wood and popping embers.

"Get down here and open this door," he bellowed, letting loose with one of the barrels, not caring whether it was close to its mark or not.

Jenny and Giles scrambled back inside and leapt onto the bed, throwing their arms tightly around each other.

"What are we going to do," sobbed Giles, clinging desperately to his sister, fearing for his very life. Jenny was sniffing and sobbing along with him, but all the while her mind was racing, thinking of ways she could protect the pair of them.

"It's me that he wants," she said finally, rubbing the tears from her eyes, giving a long hard sniff, and holding Giles out at arms length.

Staring into his eyes she continued.

"It's not you. You've done nothing wrong. He wants me, and I've got to go to him"

Giles, realising the finality of what she had said, shook his head violently.

"No!" he wailed. "No! Not you. You can't go. You mustn't"

Gripping both of his shoulders, she shook him gently but firmly to calm him down.

"It's the only way, Giles," she whispered

"At least this way we'll stand a chance."

For a moment she was silent as she waited, until she had his full attention. Then she continued.

"When I go down, and you hear me open the back door to let him in, I want you to climb out of this window and run as fast as you can to Lechlade. Do you understand?"

He nodded.

"Good," she smiled, praying that the ivy climbing up the outside wall would hold him, and not give way, sending him crashing to the ground.

Taking a deep breath she continued.

"You know where Chas lives?"

He nodded.

"Good," she smiled again, trying to instill some form of confidence into him.

"Tell him what's happened. He'll know what to do."

"But I can't leave you" he wailed, tears flowing from his eyes.

"Not with him like this. He'll kill you."

She shook her head.

"No Giles. He wont," she lied.

"He doesn't want to kill me. He just wants to frighten me. Because I told the Police what I knew. That's all."

Whether Giles believed her or not had little consequence right now. Already Jacob was loosing his patience, banging on the door again, setting Dog off barking once more.

"Get down here, you slut," he bellowed.

"If you don't, then I'm coming up there after you."

Staring deep into Giles's eyes Jenny held him firmly and whispered

"This is it. You must go now. I'm relying on you."

Those last four words were enough for Giles. If his sister was relying on him, then he must do all in his power to help her. And deep down, he knew this was the only way. Together they clung to each other for comfort, before Jenny finally pushed him away and slowly crept towards the open bedroom door. With one last pitiful look at her younger brother, she turned, pulled the white sheet tighter around her thin waif like body and disappeared from view as she slowly descended the stairs.

The final step creaked as she trod upon it and her stomach tightened into an even more severe knot. She barely breathed. She knew the end was drawing near, and prayed silently that Giles would reach the safety of her dear friend, Chas. When she was gone, at least he would see him all right. Or maybe the Dawson's. Who knows? But at least he would be safe. And that was all that mattered.

As she pulled the latch on the door, leading to the parlour, Dog was already there to greet her. Kneeling down, she flung her arms around him, burying her face deep into the course hair around his neck. If only she could remain like this for ever. Feeling warmth and comfort, from a true and faithful friend.

But she knew it could not be. Jacob was still out there. Past the back door, with shotgun in hand, waiting for her to appear.

Leaving the parlour in darkness, she crossed the room and reached the back door. Reaching down, she felt the lump of beech wood left there many weeks before, and took it in her hand.

"Jacob" she called in a shaking voice, rattling the latch and hoping to gain his full attention, giving Giles the best chance of escape.

"What?" he bellowed from beyond the door, so forceful and with such anger that she began to quake.

Taking a deep breath to calm herself, she continued.

"I'm trying to undo the door, but it's stuck."

## SEVEN

Giles, listening from the upstairs window, could hear Jacob was still at the back door and so began his descent. The ivy held his weight, but only just, and he cursed as ragged dried twigs scratched his back and arms. But soon he reached the ground, and with one final look in the direction of the rear of the house, he was off and away along the country road leading towards Lechlade.

With no more than a night shirt to keep him warm, he was already feeling the chill of the night air, and he desperately wished he had donned a pair of boots before he left, for the soles of his feet were becoming raw and bruised from small pebbles and stones that littered the way. But his own comforts were the last thing on his mind as he left the house. He was desperate to seek help, and save the pair of them from Jacob. Looking back as he ran, almost hoping for one last look at Jenny, he saw the barn well alight, and knew that soon, other people in the surrounding area would, if they were awake, see the flames and hopefully raise the alarm.

As he ran, closing the gap between himself and Lechlade, the cold air was already biting deep into his lungs, and soon he began to cough, which slowed him down even more. Eventually he had to stop, bend forward and gasp for air. The cold rawness bit deep and hard, and he grimaced as his lungs began to fill and then exhale. He willed himself to go on, for Jenny's sake as much as his own. and though he tried a few faltering steps, he knew he had to stop and take a rest.

Another child his age would have covered the distance with time enough to spare. But Giles had been a sickly child in the past, suffering frequently from colds and 'flu, and it had left his lungs weak. Such as now. He knew he should go on; for Jenny. He should force himself. But he knew he had reached his limits. There was no more he could do, and lowering himself to the ground, he sat on the roadside bank, waiting for his strength to return.

Jacob meanwhile, had tired of hammering the back door with the stock of his gun, and smashed a side window. Dog, seeing his old adversary silhouetted against the broken frame, lunged forward, as Jacob brought both barrels to bear on the poor unfortunate animal.

Jenny screamed and prayed to God in one swift second.

"Dog! Here. Come here!"

The old animal froze, torn between anger and friendship. If he had moved faster, the shot from the cartridge would have missed. But most caught him in the side of the neck as he turned to Jenny. He fell in a heap on the floor. Jenny ran to him as Jacob peered through the broken window and laughed.

"Leave him," he snarled, aiming the gun towards her, " and open that bloody door. Before I let one off at you as well."

Jenny stared down at Dog, laying motionless on the floor, and she craved to hold him close. But the sound of Jacob's voice, cold and menacing, drove her

away from her companion towards the door. As she reached it, and started

turning the key, she began to wonder. Was that the second shot he fired after

killing the policeman. Had Jacob used up the two cartridges the gun would hold.

Or had he reloaded after the earlier shot when he fired up at the bedroom

window. She could not tell. He had been outside with ample time to spare,

whilst she was climbing down the stairs. But there was a chance. A very fine

chance. And if so, how could she take advantage of it.

"Open that door," he bellowed again from outside, his patience wearing thin,

and she knew the decision she must make would have to be quick. If her

thinking was right, and the gun was empty, he may realise himself and reload.

That she could not afford to happen. She must keep him occupied while she

thought of a plan.

Again she told him the lock was stuck, and again he cursed her.

"If you don't open it now, you slut," he barked, "I'm coming through the

window."

The window. Of course. That was it. He could not control the gun and climb

through at the same time. She pleaded with him to give her more time. Crossing

the room, with beech wood in her hand, she let the sheet around her shoulders

fall to the ground and stood with her back against the wall. And there she

waited. Breathing lightly, her breasts hardly moving, through the pure white nightdress she had washed the day before. Staring down at Dog, her eyes so full of tears, she prayed that he may live. But in the semi darkness of the room, she could not see him move, and feared the worst.

Jacob grunted as he pulled himself up level with the window, and her grip tightened on the beech wood cudgel. He was breathing heavy, and even from here she could smell his stinking body. See the matted hair, the course tangled beard. Leaping flames from the barn across the way lit up parts of the room, and cast strange shadows around her, like lords and ladies leaping in some strange satanic dance. She shivered; partly from fear, partly from the cold. And so she waited.

Giles, meanwhile, had barely recovered his strength, and was still resting on the side of the road, when his eyes focused on a light, way off in the distance. At first it was no more than a flicker, like a glowing ember. But slowly it grew in size and became two. His first thoughts were to run and hide. Find somewhere safe until it had passed. But as the lights drew nearer he could hear the sound of an engine, and gradually realised a lorry or truck was approaching him, and these were the headlights. Leaping out into the center of the road, he waved his arms above his head and shouted for the driver to stop. Whoever it was, he did not care. At worst they must be able to help him in some way. At best they may even be a friend.

As the lorry shuddered to a halt, a friendly voice from inside the cab shouted out to him.

"Giles, what are you doing here?"

Immediately he recognised the voice of Chas and dashed to the open window on the driver's side of the lorry. Together they fired questions and answers at each other and it soon became clear that Chas had risen early that morning to make a round trip to Cheltenham, Chippenham and Swindon with his cattle lorry. As he looked out of his bedroom window, he had seen the glow in the sky and guessed it was Holly Bank Farm. Fortunately he had woken his neighbour, who would have called the Fire Brigade by now, and no doubt they were on their way. As he pulled Giles into the cab and across his lap into the passenger seat, he told him they had best make all haste for the farm.

"But Jacob's got a gun," argued Giles, settling down into the seat.

"We need the Police."

Chas slammed the gear stick into first and as he slipped it on into second said "No time for that now. We need to get there fast if we're to help Jenny."

Giles had to agree with that, but he still thought they were putting themselves in real danger by returning there alone.

Jenny swung the cudgel with such force that the large end caught Jacob full force in the face and sent him reeling back into the garden, crying out in pain. His nose was crushed and gushing blood, and what was once a chin now appeared to be only half a chin. Taking one last look at Dog, Jenny dashed for the door and pulled the bolt to one side. It was now or never and she prayed to God that she had hit her brother hard enough and the gun was empty. Reaching the garden gate, still with the cudgel in her hand, she flung it open and rushed out into the yard. She knew she must hide somewhere, for if Jacob were to recover, which no doubt he would soon, then he would easily out run her, even in his present condition. Her only hope was to hide up and wait for help to arrive. That was if Giles could managed to get through to Lechlade.

Her head turning this way and that, she was unsure which way to go. Flames were already leaping from the barn, high into the sky, and the heat on the far side of the yard was intense. The whole yard was alight, just like it was daylight, and she knew she must find a hiding place soon, or all her recent plans would have been for nothing. The obvious place would be the stable. She would have been safe in there, away from the fire and out of harms way. But that would be the first place Jacob would look. So where else. Desperately she looked around the yard. Of course. The fire. Already it was creeping towards the cowshed, which stood between the two barns. If only she could stand the heat she had a plan. Ripping a length of material from her cotton nightdress, she dashed across the yard, hooked the material to the corner of the door leading into the cowshed, and leaving the door slightly ajar, ran back to the safety of the stable and hid behind the door. Gasping for breath, she knelt down and waited, hoping her breathing would have slowed down before Jacob appeared.

She didn't have long to wait. A lesser man could well have died from such injuries. The bone was shattered in various pieces beyond the nose and chin.

Blood vessels were ripped apart, and many muscles did not exist any more. But they say madness can dull all pain. And this seemed to be the case with Jacob. If he was not mad in the true sense of the word, then he was certainly mad with anger. He hated his sister and he was now about to make sure she was going to pay the ultimate price.

With the gun held in both hands, he staggered through the garden gate and out into the yard. Almost mimicking Jenny earlier, his bloodied head turned from left to right, searching for her, intent on finding her and doing his worst.

Jenny shivered in the stables, and hid from sight behind the door. She dare not risk exposing herself. Not yet. She must give him time.

Already he was crossing the yard, heading first one way, then the next. Now he was near the stables. No more than ten yards away. He coughed deeply, from the blood that trickled down the inside of his throat. He grimaced, and Jenny jumped. She let out a little yelp of fear. But he did not hear her. The noise from the burning barn covered any small noises like that. Turning away, he crossed to the middle of the yard, for he had seen the small strip of material, caught on the cow shed door, and he gave what could be almost construed as a smile. The pain was excruciating, but the excitement of what he was about to do to Jenny masked any form of pain, however severe it may have been. And now, ignoring the heat from the barn, as the timbers crackled above him, and apparently unaware that the flames that were leaping across onto the cowshed roof, he pursued his quarry. With a few more steps Jenny watched him disappearing into the black void that was no more than an open doorway, and she prayed she would never see him again.

Leaving the cudgel on the floor, she rose to her feet and waited a few seconds. Once she felt it safe, she crept from the safety of the stable, out into the yard. Eyes twitching this way and that, she took one final look at the cow shed, slowly being enveloped in flames, and then, like a frightened rabbit, scurried away, out past the five bar gate and down along the road leading towards Lechlade.

She never saw Dog limping from the house that night, as she hurried through the gate. He was a pathetic site. Coat stained dark red from the dried blood about his neck. A limp that almost caused him to fall every time he moved a step forward. But being the stalwart he was, he pressed on, out into the garden and beyond. Whether he was looking for Jenny, or something else was hard to tell. His nose twitched as he sensed the air, and his ears turned from side to side as he listened. Was it the sound of the fire, cracking and popping all around him, or something more sinister. Maybe something supernatural. Something that only an animal can sense. Way beyond the understanding or the comprehension of the human soul. His course altered and now he was limping towards the cow shed. Slowly, very slowly. And no doubt every step caused him pain. But it was as though he knew Jacob was in there, and he was about to find him. It did not take long. As he neared the open doorway, as black as coal inside, with flames leaping around its edges and the timber trusses above, he appeared to ignore the heat and lowered his haunches to the ground. And there he sat, and waited. Staring into the black void beyond, as though he knew that Jacob was inside.

And so it was, when Jacob finally reappeared, having been unable to find Jenny, and being forced out by the heat, that Dog was sitting there waiting for him. As the two old enemies stared at each other, through the heat haze, the smoke and the dust, Jacob raised the gun to his shoulder and slowly took aim. Dog did not move. He merely looked at his foe with expressionless eyes, as if waiting for death to come. Jacob squeezed gently on the first trigger. There was a dull click. Pressure on the second trigger resulted in the same response. Suddenly he was aware that he had not reloaded the gun. Panic set in as he looked at Dog and saw the expression change. Anger, bitterness, hatred. All forms of emotion that had built up over the years through the cruelty he had suffered at the hands of this man. And now Jacob could see the teeth as the lips peeled back. And for the first time in many a year, he was afraid. The heat was becoming intense. he must move. But Dog blocked his path. If he ventured near the animal he knew he would be ripped to shreds. He was alone and he was trapped. Searching desperately amongst his pockets for the box containing the remaining cartridges he heard a mighty crack from above and looked up. But it was too late. Already the supporting truss above the door had given way. And now, no more than a burning black mass of oak and nails, it pinned him to the floor. He screamed as the weight crushed the skeletal bones in his body, as the heat began to shrivel his flesh, and he was still screaming, long after Dog had stood up, turned and limped away.

# EIGHT

"What a bloody mess," said the Detective Inspector to his Sergeant.

The Sergeant nodded, whilst his side kick said nothing.

The three men leant against the five bar gate, watching the local fire brigade finish off their dousing down and stowing away their pipes.

"How the hell did it happen?" he continued.

"Two of our own lads, shot down just like that."

The sergeant tried to explain what he had gleaned from "the girl", but it did little to ease the burden. Loosing one of your own was bad enough. But two, on the same night. That was bloody intolerable. How was he going to explain that away to the families?

"Where's the girl now?" he asked, screwing a dog end into the ground, making sure it was out.

"In the house," replied the Sergeant, leading the way.

The sidekick remained outside, and began to ferret around the yard. He was not the most elegant of men, but he was dedicated to his work.

Inside, the two Police men joined Sergeant Dicks, Chas, Giles and Jenny. They were seated around the table, holding mugs of tea, but not really drinking them. Jenny offered to pour the newcomers a brew, but they declined the offer and began to ask routine questions, just to unravel the mystery from the night before. Jenny was the one who could tell them the most, but after a while Chas suggested they leave her to recover, and after a few more questions, and in the inspector's own time, the three Policemen left the room.

"Dog will be all right, wont he?" Jenny asked, staring across the table into Chas's bloodshot eyes.

He nodded and said "If anyone can fix him up, then Duncan Mayhew can. He has to be the best vet in the County."

Maybe that was a slight exaggeration, but Duncan was very experienced in his own particular field, and Dog had as much chance of making a full recovery with him as he did with anyone else. Especially as Chas and Jenny had found him so soon after he left the farm, wandering down the Lechlade road towards them.

Jenny sold the farm, soon after the fire, and Harry Dawson offered her similar acreage with a few barns and cottage on his estate at a price that was well below the going rate. She accepted, of course, and along with Giles and Dog to help her, she became well know in the area as a well respected farmer. She spent many happy hours with her friend Alice, who taught her a multitude of things that a young girl growing into womanhood should know, and this would stand her in good stead in later life.

Soon after selling the farm and setting up on the Dawson estate, she married Chas. As they lay in each others arms on their honeymoon, and they made love, she found she was still a virgin. She realised, at long last, that Jacob had not managed to rape her, and for the first time in a long while, she felt pure again.